P9-DFJ-781
3 3484 00104 0580

BUCHANAN'S WAR

Also by Jonas Ward in Large Print:

Buchanan Gets Mad
Buchanan's Revenge
The Name's Buchanan

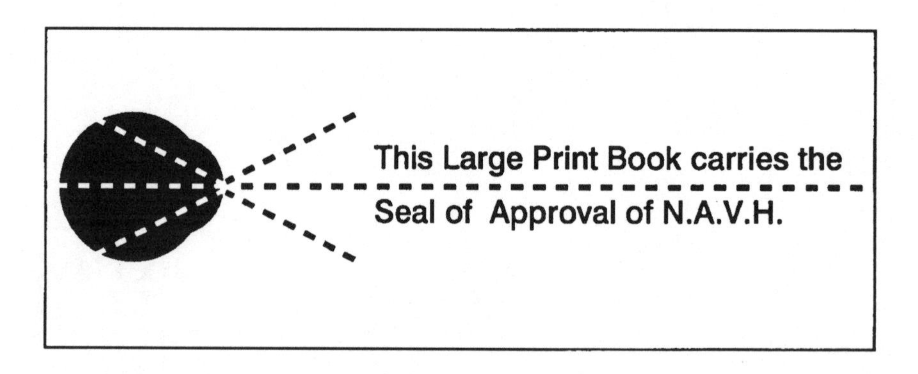

BUCHANAN'S WAR

Jonas Ward

G.K. Hall & Co.
Thorndike, Maine

All characters in this book are fictional, and any resemblance to persons, living or dead, is purely coincidental.

Published in 1997 by arrangement with
Golden West Literary Agency.

G.K. Hall Large Print Western Collection.

The text of this Large Print edition is unabridged.
Other aspects of the book may vary from the original edition.

Set in 16 pt. Bookman Old Style by Minnie B. Raven.

Printed in the United States on permanent paper.

Library of Congress Cataloging in Publication Data

Ward, Jonas, 1939–
Buchanan's War / Jonas Ward.
p. cm.
ISBN 0-7838-1878-5 (lg. print : hc)
1. Buchanan, Tom (Fictitious character) — Fiction.
2. Large type books. I. Title.
[PS3557.A715B85 1997]
813′.54—dc20 96-24241

BUCHANAN'S WAR

CHAPTER ONE

Buchanan sat on the big black horse called Nightshade and considered the situation. It was coming on dark and the couple of hundred head of Lazy M cattle were gaunt and restless and there was pursuit. Thus far, they had avoided violence, which was all to Buchanan's liking. He had signed on to recover the stolen herd, not to kill anyone.

Scott McKay strode over to him, and Buchanan got down from the saddle, all six-feet-four of him, to talk to the owner of the Lazy M. The two men made an odd contrast.

Buchanan was a gentle giant, all bone and gristle and muscle, scarred from many reluctant battles. His florid complexion and hazel eyes reflected his Scottish ancestry. McKay was short and lean with dark skin, piercing black eyes, a fierce mustache and a commanding presence.

McKay said, "There's only a half dozen greasers. We can wipe them out."

"They're Corrido's men," Buchanan replied. "Maybe even he's with 'em. You don't call them 'greasers.' You call 'em *vaqueros.* They're mighty tough people."

"They stole my cattle. They're thieves."

"Bandidos," Buchanan said. "They reckon all Texas and everything in Texas belongs to them by rights."

"Whose side are you on?" McKay demanded. "You've been talking up those greasers all the way."

"Now, McKay," Buchanan said patiently, "it's just that you don't know these people. You been up on the Canadian border fightin' Sioux and Cheyenne. These people are different."

"I don't see it. The Indians think they own the country, too."

As McKay's voice became more impatient, the two Lazy M riders who were not tending herd drew closer. Obie Deal, the foreman, was a trained cattle herder. A barrel of a man, he was stubborn and as loyal as a man could be. Hunt was easily recognized as a gun, one of the legion who roamed for hire and who never worked very hard. A slim, narrow-faced man, he was tall as a rake and not much wider.

"No use to argue, no time for it." Buchanan spoke easily. "Thing is, I know Corrido. Now you got to remember that, across the river there, is maybe Major Jones. The Rangers don't look too kindly on us goin' down to take back your cattle.

It's sort of agin' the law. Or somethin'. So — we got a war behind us, and ahead we got to find a way over the *rio*."

"We kill those damn horse thieves, then we'll worry about the Rangers." McKay closed a gauntleted fist. "By God, nobody runs on me. Nobody ever did, and nobody ever will."

Buchanan looked helplessly at Obie Deal. "Why don't you tell your boss? You know about Corrido. You know Major Jones."

The foreman had a voice like a rasping file. "It don't make no neverminds to me, Buchanan. What Scott says — that's gospel."

"Hunt?" He knew it was no good, but he had to ask.

"When I hire out, I take orders," the thin man said.

Buchanan shook his head, but McKay went on, accusing.

"I hired you to show us the way because you know this country, Buchanan. You did your job, that's okay. But now you've been buckin' me for two days. I'm beginning to have my doubts about you."

"Uh-huh." Buchanan sighed. "Well, if I was you and in a spot like this and had doubts — I'd pay the man off."

"I won't pay you a dime," McKay shouted. "You can stay and do like I say, or you can quit like a dog."

Hunt faded back a step to give his gun hand an angle. Obie Deal moved closer to his boss as though to protect him. Behind Buchanan the two herders, Madigan and Bender, dismounted and began to walk carefully toward the group.

Contrary to his practice and because he was riding a herd, Buchanan was wearing his six-gun. He would rather it was in his saddlepack, where it usually roosted. Few men would kill an unarmed person, but at this moment he was meat for the grinder in which he was caught. His mind went around, but in neither haste nor fear, considering the situation.

He had a slight edge, he thought, because they did not know what he could do. A big man, slow moving, he had not been forced to action during the foray into Mexico. They had no idea he could cut down Hunt, then seize Scott McKay and use him for a shield. In that case he would have to kill Obie Deal also, before the loyal one could interfere. Of course, this procedure might get him killed if the men behind him were prompt, but he doubted this. Madigan and Bender were only riders, cowboys, they weren't killers.

Only Hunt was a killer, he reflected. McKay might be hardheaded and wrong, but he was a decent enough man and Obie was a staunch one. None of them had taken Buchanan in as their own: Hunt was a loner, and the Lazy M men stuck together and kept to themselves. He never had had the wish to hurt people, and now didn't seem the right time to start a small war.

Meantime, it would be dangerous to make a sudden move. He slowly raised his thick arms to shoulder height and spoke in a humble voice, watching Hunt, the dangerous one.

"Yeah . . . well, what can I say?"

"Take his gun, Hunt," McKay said. "Somebody get his rifle and let him ride away. We don't need a yella hound to get home."

Hunt, disgusted by Buchanan's defeated manner, sauntered forward. Buchanan felt the men behind him relax. The thin gunslinger lifted the Colt's from the holster.

The moment the muzzle cleared, Buchanan took hold of Hunt in his two hands. He picked up the thin man and launched him like a projectile toward Obie Deal, yelling, "Catch!"

Deal put up his hands, and the force of Hunt's flying body sent him staggering backward. He tripped over a chunk of buffalo grass and went down.

Buchanan wheeled and got hold of Madigan. He rolled the cowboy toward Bender, banging their heads together so they rang like gongs. Then he kicked out a long leg and booted the six-gun from McKay's hand so that it described a neat parabola and landed in Buchanan's own fist.

"Sure hate this sort of fuss," he told them. "My pay, now, it would be a hundred and two dollars, countin' today. I'll take it in bills or in gold, any old way, Mr. McKay."

Hunt made a move and Buchanan turned the revolver toward him. McKay stood stock still, his face frozen, one emotion after the other parading in his dark eyes, struggling for composure. Obie Deal climbed to his feet, saw the pistol which Buchanan held and stopped dead.

Hunt said without raising his voice, "Reckon you want your own iron, Buchanan."

"I'd admire to have it, yes, indeed."

The gunslinger got up and walked over and extended the Colt's butt first. "You move good. You move real good. Like to see you try it with the gun some time or other."

"I ain't much for gunfights," Buchanan said. "You mind droppin' your belt for now?"

"Not at all," Hunt said. "Comes the time, my papa always says, comes the time."

"You mind payin' me off?" Buchanan asked McKay.

The cattleman hesitated, then said calmly, "I'd rather have you stay on. You just showed me somethin'."

"I apologize," the big man said. "Hate to start a ruckus. But I did my job, and I don't agree with your orders nor your notions. I'm not a Lazy M man; I didn't hire out to ride for your outfit. So let us part in peace."

Hunt said to no one in particular, "I'd let the man go with his pay, my ownself."

Again McKay hesitated. Then he reached inside his shirt and unbuckled a money belt. He counted out bills and extended them. Buchanan flipped open McKay's revolver and emptied it of bullets, then returned it to its owner. He pocketed the money without counting it.

"Fair exchange is no robbery," he remarked. "Youall better head for the river right now. Take that crossin' nearest El Paso like I told you. They won't be lookin' for you to cross there. And if Major Jones shows up, don't start nothin' with him or his Rangers."

"We heard all that before," McKay said. "Now take my advice: Stay away from the high plain and my town."

"Your town? Scottsville?"

"You heard me."

"Your town. Why, Mr. McKay, I hear some about Gabe Goodwin bein' first man on that graze."

McKay turned purple as the prairie sage. "Gabe Goodwin, my left hind foot. I'll take care of him my own way."

"You know, you ain't a bad sorta man in some ways," Buchanan told him. "Thing is, you got some *loco* notions. Like all Mexicans are no-account greasers. Indians don't have rights in land they once owned. Gabe Goodwin is somethin' you can handle quick and easy. You got a lot to learn about Texas and Texans. Believe me . . . Now, everybody just be nice and let me get aboard my horse, please. I'd purely love to go peaceable."

He backed to where Nightshade, a trained and able beast, awaited him. Never taking his eyes from the Lazy M bunch, he made a mount that seemed impossible for a man of his size and heft. He grinned at them and drew his rifle from its boot.

"So long and lots of luck," he called and put the horse into a long, circling movement which allowed him to continue to keep one eye on the group as he aimed for the Rio Grande as close to El Paso as possible. They did not make any move to grab rifles or to follow.

Indeed, McKay stood with his money belt in his hand, staring hard at the giant on the big horse as they diminished against the horizon and night came apace, his mustache drooping, indecision upon him. The herders picked themselves up dazed, not sure what it was all about.

"Damn him to hell," Obie Deal said. "If I ever see him again I'll put the boots to him."

"Better not try," Hunt said. He still held his revolver in his hand. He looked down at it, then at McKay and the Lazy M men. "Buchanan is somethin' else again, seems like. Also and otherwise — I think he's right."

"Don't you start up, now," McKay said. "I've had enough for one day."

Hunt said, "You think you had enough. Not quite, I'm afraid, not quite. Like — I'll take that money belt if you don't mind. Or even if you do mind."

He was the only man with drawn gun. They knew his reputation. Obie Deal cursed like a muleskinner, but he made no overt move. Only McKay stood stubborn, and outraged.

McKay said, "Come and get it, gunny. I saw Buchanan handle you like a baby. Come and try me."

"But, you see, I ain't Buchanan," Hunt remonstrated. The revolver spoke. The money belt flew from McKay's grasp with a hole in its buckle end. "Next one finds a gut, anybody's gut, I ain't particular."

Obie Deal picked up the belt and handed it over. "No use, boss. This one'll kill us all."

"Obie knows me some," Hunt said. He walked to his horse and hung the money belt on the saddle. "But I ain't an honest-to-goodness thief, am I Obie?"

"Not until now, you dirty rotten son."

"Not now, neither. Way I figure, Buchanan

ran one on us all. So, I take the money in advance. Too bad, I sorta like the way he handles hisself."

"Money in advance?"

"Oh, sure." Hunt slid into the saddle. "Might's well."

"For what?"

"Hell, after what happened here? You got to ask?"

"I'm askin'."

"Why, I got to kill Buchanan, that's all."

He rode off in the general direction of the river. Obie's swear words followed him until he was out of view.

McKay said, "All right. Always take your losses and go forward. Learned that in the War when I was a kid. Get the herd goin', men."

"To where Buchanan told us about?"

"That's the place. And let's move. All I need now," McKay said, "is to have those damn Rangers on my back."

The riders went to their ponies. This was their business. They know how to drive cattle. In a few minutes they had the recovered herd headed for the river. They had forgotten about Corrido — he was too far behind to catch up if they moved fast. They were doing precisely what Buchanan had advised them to do, McKay reflected — without the valuable services of the big man. And without a thousand dollars or so in cash, which Hunt had taken from him. The whole excursion was not worth the candle, he thought without heat. And they still had to get by the Rangers.

CHAPTER TWO

Buchanan, a man who enjoyed good, innocent fun, had been too long without. El Paso was jumping with all kinds of entertainment. Not so far in the past, this had been Franklin, a sleepy little border town without opportunity. It was now, with the rails and new business therefrom, a bustling, burgeoning community populated by gamblers, gunfighters, women no better than they should be and saloonkeepers galore. Prosperity and civilization had come to El Paso del Norte and environs: cattle roamed the plains to the base of the mountains; herds gathered and fattened, glutting the sparse graze; bankers, lawyers and politicians were gathered like buzzards, feasting off the multitude.

Buchanan had one hundred and two dollars and four bits. The half dollar had been his sole coin when he hired out to Scott McKay, which was the good and only reason he had taken the job. What he really wanted was a grubstake in order to hie himself to the Black Range in New Mexico, where a certain old prospector had already begun digging for the gold they would share under certain conditions: mainly, food and supplies to be furnished by Buchanan.

Now, his first consideration was his horse, and he rode into a side street livery stable, unsaddled, rubbed down Nightshade and fed a mess of oats to the big horse. There was a barbershop nearby, and he repaired into it to luxuriate in a huge wooden tub complete with almost-hot water.

He thought about McKay and the Lazy M men while soaping himself — he always thought best in a bath. Trouble, trouble, anyone going against tough old Gabe Goodwin was looking for trouble . . . McKay was a northern man, he didn't know the unreconstructed Rebels of Texas . . . Hunt, now, he could be bad, but Gabe always had a couple of fast riders with him . . . Gabe had started with a wide loop and was doing right good . . . And he was as hard-skulled as McKay, look how he had fought with his own son Pat, until Pat had hauled his stick and joined the Rangers . . . Pat, was hardheaded too, and also hotheaded, which Gabe was not . . . Gabe's way was to wear a man down with plain, natural stubbornness until there was no getting along with him whatsoever . . . Oh, McKay would have himself a buster of a time running Gabe off the plains around Scottsville, whatever that was, certainly a town that had not been named after any northern cattleman like McKay . . . Maybe McKay had settled there because it was already Scottsville, believing it to be a good omen . . . He'd need a lot of luck, going against Gabe Goodwin.

It seemed kind of dumb . . . Far as Buchanan knew, both McKay and Gabe were as honest as need be . . . Not really, truly square because both were out to grab and hold onto things, but not real crooked, neither . . . Good sense would seem to auger that they get together and live peaceable and share the graze and the water between the Lazy M and the GG brand . . . But then it was noticeable that them that wants a lot has a lot of trouble gettin' along with each other . . . Or anybody else.

Well, it wasn't any skin off Buchanan's elbow. He was tender with the yellow soap on his scars. He'd had enough trouble lately; things just hadn't rolled his way. He was no great gambler, but it seemed to him that the pendulum of luck should be swinging back his way. Maybe, if he got up into the Black Range with some grub, he and the old man would strike it rich . . .

He got up, bending his head to keep from banging it on the ceiling, grabbed a towel and wiped himself dry. He put on a clean shirt and wrinkled pants from his bedroll and went out. He sat down and had a shave and a trim at the hands of an Italian barber. Thus refreshed, he toted his bedroll back to the stable, made sure that Nightshade was all right and headed for the main stem and the bright lights.

He listened to the music from the honkatonks, the drone of the dealers, the spinning wheels, the clack of poker chips and the cries of dance hall girls, but he was hungry first, hungry for vittles. He went into Considine's Saloon, which he knew of old as a combined restaurant and bar without wheels of chance — just a nice, businessman's eatery. He ordered six eggs, a thick steak well done, mashed potatoes and apple pie and ice cream. The best thing about a town getting civilized, he thought, was that it brought ice cream to the people. He sat with his back to the wall through long habit. Bill Considine spotted him and came from the saloon, an old-timer in a gambler's frock coat and string tie, grinning.

"Hey, Tom."

"Light and have one," Buchanan said. "I was just about to yell for a beer."

"Got the good Mex stuff on ice. We finally got us some ice. Town's gettin' mighty big."

"I reckon," Buchanan said. "Maybe too big?"

"Sure enough too big. We got a Marshal and deputies and a Ranger office and everything. You know a nice quiet place to open up a joint?"

"What about Scottsville?"

Considine waited until a beefy barkeep had brought the beer in a pitcher and a bottle of whiskey for his own pleasure. Then he said, "What's that mean, Tom?"

"Just heard about it is all. Guess it was atop my mind."

"Then you ain't seen Gabe Goodwin? Or Pat?"

"Nope." He was about to say he had just got into town but decided his past movements might better remain private. "I ain't aimin' to see Gabe."

"I forgot. You and him had it."

"Just don't want to be around him," Buchanan said. "You say one thing, Gabe says another. Monotonous."

"I know, but he's an old sidekick of mine." Considine scowled. "Fella named McKay is givin' him a lot of trouble, and he thought Pat oughta come home. Pat ain't about to."

"I know."

"That Scottsville ain't a nice, quiet place. It's a little old hot place, Gabe tells me. Got a fella name of Vic Carmer runnin' a gamblin' spot and saloon. You ever heard of him?"

"Never did." Buchanan drank a pint of beer in one thirsty swallow.

"It ain't like Gabe to worry none. Must be

on account of his girl."

"Is Mary home? Thought she settled back East."

"She's home. Never did hear Gabe go on like tonight. Pat's out on a scout or somethin' for Major Jones. Gabe's at the hotel, the Baldwin House."

"Don't tell me, I don't wanta know. I'm headin' clear outa Texas." He did not mention the Black Range; there were too many gold seekers up there now. "That Mary, she was a wild little thing. Pretty as a speckled hen but wild."

"That's why Gabe sent her back to relatives in the East. Says she's a beauty now, all right. Never did hear Gabe talk so much."

"We're all gettin' older," Buchanan said, who was years younger than either Gabe or Billy Considine. He finished the beer, and the waitress, a pretty Mexican girl with a big smile, came bearing a tray. He grinned at her, and the girl dimpled, curtsied and rolled her eyes.

Considine said, "Hate to admit it, though. Hate to see Gabe losin' his nerve, talkin' so much."

"This McKay must be *muy hombre*, huh?" Buchanan speared an egg, put it in his mouth, added mashed potatoes and slashed off a hunk of steak. He swallowed, drank beer, bit at the meat. "Good grub you got here always, Billy."

"You're the one can stack it away," Considine said, "Man, you're as big as a horse, and you eat like one."

"But not often enough." Buchanan plowed straight on through the meal.

"Well, it seems this McKay, he's got plenty money, and Gabe, he puts it all back into the GG or gambles it away. He always was a sucker for cards. So McKay, he hires guns. Like he's got a fella named Hunt. Gabe says he's pizen."

"Hunt? Bad man, huh?"

"Gabe says, and you know Gabe. He ain't personally scared of nothin'. This Hunt must be real bad."

Buchanan's eyes were on the door. He sighed and said, "If Hunt's so awful bad, you better duck outa the way. Here he comes right now."

The thin gunman walked straight to the table. He nodded. "Buchanan."

"I don't ever carry a gun in town," Buchanan said. He ate the last egg. "You wanta light and have somethin'?"

"Nope."

"You sure?"

"I'm plenty sure." Hunt stared at Considine. "You better move, old man."

The saloonkeeper said, "Like you say." He got up and slowly walked into the bar.

Hunt said, "I remembered about you and

the way you don't wear your iron in town."

"Matter of keepin' the peace." Buchanan leaned back, hooking one foot around a table leg. Hunt was wearing two guns, tied low.

"Thing is, you made me look bad," Hunt said. "Made everybody look bad. Lazy M don't take it so good."

"Self-defense. Any court of law would leave me off."

Hunt said, "Ain't much for the law myself. Thought you and me could have it out among ourselves."

"You got the guns." The two other men in the room were going out the door, leaving their unfinished meals. Hunt's voice had a chilling effect even when raised; his monotone was a litany of death.

"Oh, I'm goin' to give you a gun."

"But I don't want a gun," Buchanan said. "The Rangers are around, and that Major Jones, he's strict. He don't like guns unless he's holdin' them."

"We can worry about that later." Hunt put his right hand on the butt of his Colt's and bent a knee. Very gingerly, he removed his left-handed revolver and placed it on the floor. He straightened up and said, "I'm not comin' near you again. I'm goin' to slide that one along the floor. I'll give you plenty time to pick it up."

"Supposin' I don't pick it up?"

"Then I'm goin' to drill you. Not to kill, not this time. I'm goin' to accidentally shoot you in the right hand. That'll be a sort of insurance, you see, against next time."

Buchanan put both hands on the table. They resembled calla hams. "Well, you go right ahead. It's your party."

"I'll enjoy it. And later on, some place, some time, I'll finish the job. Now — here's your gun."

Hunt had to look down to get his toe against the Colt's on the floor. It was a split second only, but it was what Buchanan had been waiting for. As toe of boot reached gun, Buchanan's foot sent the table flying.

At that moment, the waitress came through the door with the ice cream. She screamed, tripped and threw the tray. The confection slopped along the floor as Buchanan rose to attack behind the shield he had provided himself. His boot plopped into the ice cream. He waved his arms to regain balance and did a fast turn, swinging one hand against Hunt's head.

The slap of the big hand sent Hunt reeling and spinning. He drew his gun, however, and danced as though to music, seeking his target.

A young man flew from the bar. He had a long-barreled Colt's in his hand. He caught Hunt from the side, laying the muzzle against his head. Only Hunt's sombrero saved him from a fractured skull as he went down, his own gun loosed from his grasp.

The young man said, "Hold it, Tom." He was a tall young man, tanned and handsome, and he wore the badge of the Texas Rangers.

Buchanan said, "Sure glad to see you, Pat."

"Don't be," Pat Goodwin said, motioning toward the bar from which he had just appeared.

"Oh-oh," Buchanan said, wiping the sole of his boot on the checkered tablecloth. "Uh — how are you, Major?"

Major John B. Jones was a slight figure, weighing no more than a hundred and thirty pounds. He had to look up at Buchanan. He had black hair and eyes and fair skin. He had the thin nostrils of a thoroughbred horse. He was very neat and very polite — and very dangerous when aroused. It was apparent that he was not happy now.

"Buchanan, you're under arrest."

"For what?"

"Disturbing the peace and suspicion of just about anything in the book," the major said.

"I didn't start this rangdoodle," Buchanan protested. He had visions of a fine which would cut deeply into his grubstake. "Ask Billy. Ask the waitress."

"You're into it," Major Jones replied. "And

I have information that you were involved in a matter of invasion of our neighbors to the south. And I remember that you once drove a herd of cattle through a certain ford where this very evening another such herd managed to slip over into Texas. Is that true, Goodwin?"

Pat had disarmed Hunt and was getting him to his feet and attaching handcuffs. "Er — not to my knowledge, sir."

"But your knowledge is limited, is it not? Otherwise, you would have been on the job to prevent the incursion of said herd."

Pat said tonelessly, "Yes, sir. Whatever you say, sir."

"Can you be trusted to take these two men into custody and cast them into durance vile?" Major Jones asked in the most pleasant tone.

"Yes, sir. But handcuffs won't go 'round Buchanan's wrists, sir, if you remember."

"I remember very well. Yes, indeed." Jones smiled at Buchanan. There was no humor in the grimace. "I think Buchanan will go along, however. He is, by his own assertion, a law-abiding, peaceable citizen."

"Oh, sure," Buchanan said, recognizing defeat.

"Besides, Trooper Goodwin, he is your friend. If he escaped you would be in worse trouble than you are now. If that is possible."

"Yes, sir," Pat said.

Major Jones made a priestly gesture. "Go with God."

Buchanan had to support Hunt as they went out the door. He said, "I never got my ice cream."

Pat stuck the guns he had gathered into the belt around his lean waist. "That's just too damn bad, Tom."

"The major is sure o'nery tonight. Why didn't you guard that crossing?"

"My old man held me up."

"Then he did find you?"

"He found me. Had another big hooraw with him. He wants me to quit and go home. I ain't about to while he's alive, the old devil."

Buchanan gestured toward the other prisoner. "This here is one reason he wants you. Name of Hunt."

"So this is the *hombre?* Maybe we ought to let him try to escape or somethin'."

"I'm agin' backshootin'," Buchanan said. "But I am gettin' weary of this galoot. He keeps tryin' to kill me."

"We'll put him under the jail," Pat said gloomily. "The major is ready to put somebody, anybody, under the jail."

"Maybe you oughta quit and go back to Scottsville."

"Not me. My old man is bad enough. She's worse."

"Your sister?"

"Her, too. But that McKay gal! Man, you never heard such carryin's on."

"Carryin' on?" He had not known McKay possessed a daughter.

"Just because her father and my father are feudin'."

"Oh. I see."

"The hell with 'em. The hell with Scottsville."

The last cobweb seemed to have cleared from Hunt's addled brain. "What the hell's goin' on here? Who hogtied me? I'll kill the man who put bracelets on me."

"Aw, shut up," Buchanan said. "I'm gettin' real tired of you, Hunt. Always interruptin' a man."

Hunt said, "I'll interrupt you, all right. I'll interrupt your heartbeat."

Pat Goodwin shook the prisoner, almost sending him to the walk. People were staring, but nobody made a comment or even directed a hard stare. The Rangers under Major Jones had grown tremendously powerful and tough.

Pat said, "Let's just go to the hoosegow. I'm sorry, Tom, but you see how it is."

"Yeah. I remember how it was, too."

He walked along, remembering. It was about a year ago up in Mason County where there was a settlement of people of German descent who had not joined the Confederacy in the war of many years ago. Certain

Texans, who called themselves "Americans" and called the Union sympathizers "goddam Dutch," had never forgotten. Buchanan had appeared in the midst of a murderous feud.

His own sympathies had been with neither side, but when a gang of Americans, self-styled, shot an unarmed man named Dan Hoester and when wild shots flew into a hotel occupied by women and children, Buchanan had outed with his rifle and cut down the killer and a *compadre*.

A week later, a Ranger attempted to arrest Buchanan for his deed. He was a large Ranger named Wale, and Buchanan had disarmed him, roughed him up and sent him to Major Jones with a message that it would have been far better for the commandant to have been in Mason City himself rather than over in Cold Springs on a cold trail, thus perhaps preventing the murder of an innocent person.

Major Jones had looked up Buchanan, and they had exchanged a few unpleasantries. It so happened that the "Dutchmen" were not people without influence, and the Rangers had been restrained by the Governor of Texas from taking action against their defender. The major would never in this world forget the incident.

They came to the jail, which was not the sturdy El Paso city pen but merely a room in the rear of a single-storied frame building which housed Ranger Headquarters. Hunt, fully recovered, his hands free, took one look around the place of incarceration and snickered. There was one other prisoner, a brawny Negro with a scarred face and a broken nose. He was, Buchanan recognized, a prizefighter named Coco Bean, a man of enormous strength and skill.

In the outer office was Sergeant Wale, of all people. He still bore a few marks of his last encounter with Buchanan, and he now wore a wide grin as he made the necessary entries in the book.

Pat Goodwin said, "No monkey business, Wale. Tom's a friend of mine."

"Any friend of yours — is in trouble right now," Wale said. "Right in back with the others, Buchanan. You get no special favors here."

"I'd just as soon be with them as with you. They don't smell of skunk," Buchanan told him cheerfully.

"I'll skunk you before we're through."

Buchanan turned to Pat. "I dunno. I'm the most peaceable fella in the world, but more people are threatenin' to do me in than if I was a born fighter. It don't make sense."

Pat said, "I'll be around. Take it easy, the major will be here pretty soon, he's collectin' his mail and telegraph messages and all."

Buchanan went into the room which served as a jail. He heard the door slam and the heavy bar fall behind him. Hunt and Coco Bean were in a corner. Hunt stopped talking as soon as he saw Buchanan. The Negro came to the center of the room and spoke in soft, slurred tones.

"Man tellin' me you a fighter. Says you a real good fighter. You wanta fight me, mister?"

"Oh Lord, how long, how long?" mourned Buchanan. "No, Coco, I don't want to fight you."

"You knows me? You seen Coco fight?" The man had been hit around the head many times. He was not quite punch-drunk, but he was a bit simple.

"I saw you."

"Then you scairt of Coco."

Hunt was laughing silently. The gunny figured to make an ally of Coco, Buchanan realized. There were windows in the room, boarded over, but still ground-floor exits if they could be pried open. Coco was ridged with muscle.

Buchanan said, "I didn't say I wouldn't fight you. I said I didn't want to."

He took one long step forward. He feinted with his left. He crossed a right so quickly that Coco never saw it coming. He hit the black man in the midriff. It was like punching a washboard made of especially hard zinc. Coco pulled back his lips, displaying a veritable rainbow of shimmering white and gold.

"Now that there is a mighty fine punch, mister."

"Just call me Buchanan." His knuckles hurt. No man had ever withstood that wallop to the midsection. It was, he ruminated, simply not his day nor his evening.

Coco lifted his left hand, elbow close to chest, advancing his left foot, shuffling, weight distributed, right hand held low. He moved toward Buchanan's left in the prescribed manner of the pugilist, defending against the more lethal right-hand blow of the opponent. He slid in and deposited a ringing left alongside Buchanan's head.

"Now that's a mighty good punch, too," Buchanan said.

Coco's eyes widened; for a moment he hesitated. He felt the same as had Buchanan; his hook usually deposited his adversary on the seat of his pants. There stood Buchanan, arms at his sides, smiling at him.

A right fist suddenly slapped hard against Coco's left biceps. Alarmed, he retreated. Buchanan's hammerlike smash caught him on the forearm. Coco's left began to lack feeling, it was becoming numb. He delivered a good right lead to the neck.

Buchanan gained in spirits. At least he

had something concrete to tackle, a real challenge minus gunfire, something he could come to grips with. Amazingly swift for a man of his bulk, he came closer. He grabbed Coco in a headlock. He spun around. Coco's heels flew so that Hunt had to duck lest he be decapitated.

While he was bending low, it occurred to Hunt that he had a stake in the proceedings. He reached out a boot and put a toe in the path of the whirling Buchanan.

Still whirling, Buchanan's feet became entangled. In order to keep from falling, he had to let go of Coco. The prizefighter's bulk hurtled through the air as if shot out of a cannon. He struck precisely in the middle of the boarded window. Coco's weight was too much for the wooden panel. It burst into a dozen splintered bits.

Coco went down like a half-empty sack of potatoes. Buchanan put out his hands as he fell against the wall opposite the broken barrier.

Hunt took three jumps and dove. He went head first through the aperture and out into an alley.

The bar of the door slammed back, and Wale bustled into the room with drawn gun. Behind him, Pat stared over his shoulder. Buchanan rested his back against the wall and pointed.

"Hunt went thataway," he muttered.

Wale rushed to the window, leaned out and fired two shots. Then he pulled his head back and said, "This'll get you ten years at Huntsville, Buchanan."

"For what?" Pat Goodwin demanded.

"For lettin' that killer get away. Didn't we just get a message there was a riot in Scottsville? Ain't Hunt one of the hard cases hired by McKay? Wasn't Buchanan reported to be with McKay and Hunt below the border?"

From the doorway the calm, even voice of Major Jones said, "Be quiet, Wale. We have troubles enough without your maundering . . . Goodwin, I have an assignment for you, and this time you had better carry it out. You know Scottsville?"

"Yes, sir."

"Then you will go there at once by horse and by stage, as swiftly as possible. You will stop what appears to be a riot between two factions."

"But my father . . . The riot is between McKay's Lazy M people and my father's GG men."

"Yes," the major said. "I know."

"But how can I act in such a case?"

"I wonder," Jones said.

"But my old man . . . my father . . . he's not even there. He's in El Paso."

"We are aware of that fact. You do have a sister named Mary, do you not?"

"Well, sure, but . . ."

"Then you'd better get home and keep her quiet. Our information is that she started the whole thing. Hurry on, Goodwin. And if you don't succeed, you may wire me your resignation. No use coming all the way back to El Paso."

Buchanan watched his young friend with gravity and some concern. Pat was obviously struggling with himself. He had joined the Rangers with the best intentions. He had thought to separate himself from his unruly and sometimes slightly unlawful father and to take up the humdrum way of law and order. He had made this move in good faith.

Now he was being bullied. He was being ordered into an impossible situation. Major Jones was not only pulling the old "one riot, one Ranger" gaff, he was sending Pat against his own flesh and blood with a manifestly unfair ultimatum.

Pat said, "I'll go to Scottsville, all right." He was unpinning his badge. "But not under those orders. I won't have to wire my resignation, Major. Here's your tin, and you know what you can do with it."

Wale yelled, "Shall I arrest him, Major? Shall I throw him in with these other ones?"

Major Jones accepted the badge. "What ever for? Wale, you tax me, you really do. Those sergeant strips are fading, Wale.

Goodwin, your resignation is accepted. I imagine you'll want to be leaving at once."

Pat hesitated. "About Tom Buchanan. You know he didn't do anything against the law."

"Just run along, Goodwin," the major said. "I have plans for Mr. Buchanan."

Pat said, "When you get out, Tom, I'll be on the GG. If you need a job or anything . . . you know it's yours."

"Thanks," Buchanan said. "I think I'll stay away from your old man, if you don't mind."

"Well, the offer's open. So long." Without another word to the major or the sergeant, Pat Goodwin stalked out of the Ranger Headquarters.

Buchanan said, "I dunno if you noticed, you men, but while you were gabblin' your other prisoner decamped."

Wale rushed to the window again, but Major Jones lifted a shoulder and smiled.

"He wasn't important. As for you, Buchanan, I would have words, in private. Come, Wale, go back to your desk before somebody steals it."

The major closed the door behind the flustered sergeant. He was fingering the badge rejected by young Goodwin. He fixed his dark eyes on Buchanan.

"The judge will fine you, probably put you in jail for a while on my say-so."

"You reckon?" Buchanan had been in jail

before, and he did not enjoy it.

"That's the way it is," Major Jones said.

"I don't reckon you'd mention it unless you had a proposition," Buchanan said. "Fellas like you, they always have somethin' on their minds. The answer has got to be — no, thanks."

"Don't be hasty. The El Paso jail stinks badly and is noted for its bedbugs."

"I've been around worse than bedbugs lately."

"Nothing personal, I hope."

"You like it, you can have it." Buchanan was growing angry. He seldom allowed himself such luxury, but Major Jones was getting to him. He had never liked Jones, not any more than he cottoned to bedbugs, and he feared he was to be deprived of his hard-earned grubstake.

"You could listen," the Ranger suggested.

"I been listenin'. All I hear is bad news."

"About Scottsville. I really didn't want young Goodwin to go there in an official capacity."

"You got a fine way of showing it."

"It worked, did it not?" Major Jones smiled. "He's gone to help his family, hasn't he?"

"And maybe get killed. Hunt and them are a bad lot."

"Yes. Therefore I must send a Ranger up there. But I have other problems. I cannot spare a man."

"Tell your troubles to the judge," Buchanan suggested.

"I could do that easily enough. In fact, I need not see the judge." He turned the badge so that the lamplight caught it and reflected a tiny beam.

"Oh, no you don't," Buchanan said. "I've got plans."

"After you get out of jail?"

"This is blackmail," Buchanan said. "You're supposed to be an officer of that great body of men, the Texas Rangers. And here you are, blackmailin' me."

"There's going to be a lot of trouble at Scottsville. It would be a challenge to a man like you."

"It would, would it? Look, I've already got Hunt out to kill me. And your other good old boy prisoner, Coco, he's out to beat up on me. Now you want a whole countryside to be out to get me all at once."

"As I said, a big challenge."

"I'm being challenged by experts, as it is."

"You can renew your acquaintance with McKay."

"Who wants to — I can what?"

"I'm not at all certain that McKay is altogether guilty in this feud, this incipient range war," Jones said deliberately. "Gabe Goodwin is a sudden man. Mary Goodwin is a strange girl with masculine notions. These people are Texans, Buchanan. You're a Texan — East Texas to be sure, but a Texan. I am personally from South Carolina. I'm not born and bred. You might do your home state a good service." He paused and smiled. "And you will certainly be doing a favor for the Rangers — and for me."

Buchanan swallowed hard, then said, "Major, I am no lawman. I'm not a crook, I never stole anything in my life. But I've been here and there and around and about, and the law is sort of different in different places, and I don't always understand it. Nor believe in it."

"That is just what it takes to obtain a solution to what is happening around Scottsville," Jones said. "A man with a Texas point of view, a man who will act as he thinks is correct for the good of the commonwealth."

"Lordy me," Buchanan said. "You make it sound real important."

"It is important." Major Jones held out the badge. "You can take the oath from Sergeant Wale and draw expenses up to fifty dollars."

"Fifty dollars?"

"You'll want to use your own arms, but you'll need ammunition and traveling expenses," Jones said. "Report to me here by telegraph when possible, otherwise by mail. I expect big things of you, Buchanan."

Fully conscious that he was being taken

in and by an expert, Buchanan tentatively took the badge into his huge paw. A thought struck him, and he grinned.

"Did you say Sergeant Wale will swear me in?"

"That's right, I have an errand to perform, and I am already late."

Buchanan said, "Lead on, Major . . . sir."

They went into the office. Wale was sitting rigidly behind the desk. He glared at Buchanan with open dislike.

Major Jones said, "Sergeant, you will swear Buchanan into the Rangers, please. I will see you later in the evening. Good night — and good luck, Trooper Buchanan."

"Thank you, sir," the big man said. He was beginning to enjoy his new role. He watched Jones depart and turned on Wale. "Now you just get out the book or whatever and be a good boy. You, I can handle. And the way things have been goin', would I ever love to handle you again!"

Wale said, "The major has lost his ever-lovin' mind . . ."

He looked into Buchanan's eyes and broke off. He said, "Just raise your right hand."

Buchanan repeated the oath of office. Then he pinned the badge to his vest. It looked mighty strange glittering there. He said, "Well, you lose a Ranger, you gain a

Ranger. Now, about the expense money. Seventy-five dollars."

"Seventy-five dollars? You crazy too?"

"Expenses. To get to Scottsville. Put it on your book."

Wale relaxed. "Ah, so you're goin' to Scottsville? Now that's different. Here's your money. Like the major said, lots of luck. I hope they shoot you in the gut so you can suffer more — 'cause you're sure goin' to get it in that hell hole. Scottsville, eh? Makes me feel a lot better."

"That's good," Buchanan said. "I'd hate to see you upset much. You're ugly enough as is."

He went out of the headquarters. He started toward the livery stable. He knew it would be better to get out of El Paso before Major Jones learned that he had upped the ante on his expenses.

An extremely dark shadow came out of an alleyway. Coco Bean fell into step.

"I thought you'd be out of town by now," Buchanan said.

"Oh, nossir. You and me, we didn't finish our fun. Never let nothin' unfinished is my rule."

Buchanan said, "I'm goin' for my horse and my gear. In that gear is a big, bad Colt's .45. You start any trouble with me, Coco, and I'll put holes in you that won't stop bleedin' for a week. I'm now an officer of the law. I don't fistfight for fun. I am a serious lawman."

"You jined up?"

"You might say that." He showed Coco the badge.

Coco said, "I got me a hoss. I can ride, too. Been a cowhand in my day. I'll just go along with you until you ain't a lawman anymore."

"That'll be a long ride." Yet it added another amusement to a bad day. The idea of having Coco along on the journey to Scottsville was appealing.

"Unfinished," Coco said. "Nobody ever handled me like you did in there. Got to see if it was a accident."

Buchanan said, "Okay. Raise your right hand."

"Don't you hit me no sneak punch."

"Raise your hand."

Coco was wary, but he complied. Buchanan mumbled a few words, then said, "Now you're a deputy Texas Ranger. I just swore you in."

"I didn't hear no cuss words."

"You won't. I don't cuss much. You're my assistant. If you ride with me you got to be useful."

"I won't handle no guns. I'm skeered of guns. Always was. Folks get killed foolin' with guns."

"You're absolutely right," Buchanan said.

"Bear it in mind. You are a Texas Ranger without a gun."

"You sure that's legal?"

"If it ain't, we can worry about it later. You want to ride along with me?"

"I sure do. I ain't never seen a man tough as you. Like to find out just how tough you mought really be."

"Then come on, and don't be makin' trouble." They walked along the street, turned a corner and came to the livery stable.

CHAPTER THREE

Pat Goodwin swayed with the motion of the stage to Scottsville. The countryside rolled by, plains and mountains ascending from the flatlands. It was all too familiar.

He remembered his mother, a smiling woman who had turned away the bombast of his father with a shrug, always attending to the primitive ranch house and her two children. He had loved his mother. It was said that he resembled her while his sister Mary was precisely like his father. This was at least superficially true. Pat was earnest, always trying but never quite succeeding at learning exactly who he was. Mary knew she was Gabe Goodwin's daughter, wild, wooly and barely curried.

He thought of Linda McKay, daughter of Scott McKay, an only child. She would have none of him because her father and Gabe hated one another. They fought, those two, over land which, truth to tell, did not belong to either. It had been wrested from the Comanche and Apache and held by force. It was government graze, held on fragile lease. Goodwin had been first. McKay had come down from the north with his money and his ambitions and had moved in, legally enough but with high-handed and overbearing demeanor which set Gabe's teeth on edge. The stupid part of it, Pat thought, was that there happened to be grass and water enough for everybody.

It was Pat's oft-reiterated statement of this last fact which had caused the final break between Gabe and himself. Actually, Gabe was well aware that there was enough for McKay and himself, but he had noted, at the top of his loud voice, that Pat had not mentioned the subject to him before he got involved with Linda McKay, that "female limb of Satan," as he often described her. Gabe's stand was simplicity itself: He had been first in the country, and anyone who dared flout him and GG Ranch was an emissary of the devil ripe to be sent headlong back to where he belonged, in hell.

And there was the third factor, Vic Carmer, who had come to town about the same time as Scott McKay and who people thought might be an ally of the Lazy M owner. Nobody really knew anything about Carmer for sure, though. He proclaimed neutrality; he was a silent, mysterious, delicately handsome man from nowhere. He opened the first gambling place in his saloon, and they said his games were honest — but he prospered amazingly well for a square gambler. Pat thought of him, with dislike, as a lady's man. Both Linda McKay and his crazy sister Mary had seemed to enjoy his company. They said he was a "gentleman, with perfect manners."

It was from all this that Pat had severed himself after being rejected by Linda. Now that he was returning, he wondered why. There would be no bells ringing, no dancing in the streets, no fatted calf for the prodigal. His father would welcome him, but only because the old man had the wind up.

Truthfully, that was why he was coming home. Gabe was a loud old man but he was, after all, Pat's father; and he had never seen the toughness scratched, much less shattered, as it seemed to be now. Gabe had always been as brave as he was loud, an optimist with full confidence in his power to survive. It could not be only fear of Hunt and his ilk; Gabe had handled fast guns all his life, and on the GG he had Dungan, a proven quick draw, and Galloway, Gomez and Perry, all hard men. No, there was something underneath it all that had Gabe worried, something Pat had not waited to learn in his haste to get to the ford across the Rio Grande, to which he had come too late to put a spoke in the wheel of Scott McKay.

It had also led to the displeasure of Major Jones and his dismissal, Pat thought lugubriously. If he had made good, he might have been able to wrangle a company of Rangers to Scottsville to get at the bottom of the trouble. True, they were busy fighting organized outlaws and Indians, but it could have been arranged if he had had the influence. He had failed, and now he was going up the last grade in this rickety old stagecoach, the horses straining in the harness to carry him along, the only passenger, to a dead-end destination.

The stage topped the rise. Scottsville lay there, truly a one-street town lined with business establishments of no great distinction. People built behind the stores and livery stable. Carmer lived over his saloon, the only real two-storied building in town, all the others sporting false fronts — dismal, unpainted, rickety. At the Wells Fargo office, Pat crawled out of the uncomfortable boxlike stage and caught his bedroll as it was flung down by a driver who hated this run to no place, from whence he would turn around and go back to El Paso.

Gabe Goodwin said, "So you come back after all."

He was a gaunt man, stoop-shouldered and bearded. He had married late; he was sixty, and there was gray in his hair. He had deep, hooded eyes and a wide, mobile mouth. He was not a smiler; his facial expression was dour. He wore range clothing that was ill-kept, not very clean. Only his tooled boots and rich Stetson were badges of his position as a big rancher.

"You must have got my wire — you're here," Pat said. It was a typical meeting between the two.

Fred Masters, the sheriff friendly to Gabe and GG, an ineffective but decent man, came from the Wells Fargo office with outstretched hand. "Glad to see you, Pat. Need you around here."

"Thanks, Fred." He was looking down the street to where Carmer's saloon, newly painted, stood like a solid monument against the tacky row of Scottsville's frame buildings. Mary Goodwin was swinging her way toward them.

She never just walked, she always moved as though on springs. She was tall and well shaped, not really pretty but with huge, bright eyes and long lashes, which prevented people from noticing her plainness. She wore jeans, as always.

She called, "So you got here without being lost. Nice work, brother."

"I had a guide." He and Mary never did get along.

"The buckboard's at the livery," she said. Her gaze went up and down the street. It was late in the afternoon. "But maybe we ought to eat at Lin Chee's. My cooking seems to upset people."

"She can't bile water without scorchin' it," Gabe said, managing a grin. He had a soft spot for his daughter even when he criticized her, as he criticized everything and everyone. "Even Lin Chee cooks better."

"What happened to Buster?" Pat asked. "He could make anything taste good, even skunk stew."

Gabe's voice changed; he actually lowered it. "Buster got hisself shot. Only the bullet was meant for me."

"Buster?" The old cook was as harmless as a pet kitten. "That's really rotten."

"I'll tell you about it." Gabe was distraught now, as he had been in El Paso. "Let's go get some vittles."

There was no one on the street at suppertime. They walked past Carmer's place, and the proprietor emerged from the doorway. He wore his immaculate black-and-white costume with grace. He removed his hat and bowed.

"Good evening, folks. I am glad to see you home again, Pat . . . Miss Mary, you look lovely, as always."

Gabe Goodwin grunted, and Pat lifted a hand in greeting. But Mary actually blushed. It was hard to believe; she was not that kind of girl. But she colored to her neckerchief, and Pat was suddenly fully aware of the blush and what it implied. Mary was in the game with both feet. Mary

Goodwin and Linda McKay were both after Vic Carmer's favor.

Gabe led the way across the street to Lin Chee's restaurant, a room with four tables attached to a kitchen and, beyond the kitchen, a laundry, where Lin Chee eked out some kind of living washing dirty clothes. The eatery always smelled of soap, incense and things boiling, but it was the only place in town. Lin Chee and his diminutive, silent wife kept front and back windows open when weather permitted, but to Pat the atmosphere was just barely passable for the time it took to gulp a quick meal.

Gabe made a fuss about a table and had one put so that he could sit with his back to the wall and look out both front and rear windows. He then ordered food for them all, an old habit that angered Pat but which Mary accepted with uncharacteristic weakness. Lin Chee went away on flapping, heelless slippers.

Gabe leaned forward and said, in a voice much lower than usual but still louder than most voices, "If McKay was to home I'd know how to figure. But him and that Hunt bein' off to Mexico after them stolen beeves — it's plumb aggavatin'. Who in tarnation else wants to kill me?"

"You're not the most popular man in the county," Pat said. "But kill you? Why should McKay even try to bushwhack you?"

"That's what I'm askin' you, goldern it."

"There are GG men still around," Mary said. "We had a fight in town the other night. That's the riot you heard about, Pat. Our boys and the Lazy M crowd. Sheriff Masters sent the wire for help. He's yellow, as you know."

"Where was he?"

"In the hills looking for outlaws who rustled some of our prime stock — that's what he says," Mary replied. "If it was me, I'd start cutting down on every Lazy M man and beast I could find. The only way to beat them is to wipe them out."

"You are crazy as a bedbug, gal," Gabe said. "Fred Masters is our friend, and you can't just kill people outa hand no more. The Rangers would be here pronto."

"Besides which, it's not nice," Pat said with irony not unnoticed by his sister.

She said, "You run away, that's your answer. Now that you're back with all that police experience, I suppose you'll find out who killed Buster and stole our cattle?"

"You two stop clawin' at each other, now," Gabe said. He looked at Pat. "Fred and Carmer and some others think it was Injuns. There ain't no Injuns out; I checked with the Army post."

"Where did the shot come from?" Pat asked.

"You know that grove of trees eastward of the house? I dusted over there fast. I found this." He rolled an empty cartridge on the table.

It was bottle-shaped, and the mark of the hammer on its base was slightly off-center. "Winchester? Remington? Who could tell?" Pat asked.

"Remington, the new one everybody's got," his father said positively. "Most pop'lar rifle around. Could belong to anybody — 'ceptin' an Injun. No redskin's got one yet."

"Buster was shot with this?"

"Funny thing about that," Gabe said. "Seemed to me to be . . ."

There was no sound except for a "thwack." Gabe straightened up and sighed. He fell sideways toward Pat. Mary screamed, an unearthly keening sound. Lin Chee's wife came running. A red splotch began to grow on Gabe's shirt. He grunted and seemed to be trying to talk, but no coherent words came to Pat's ears as he supported the body. He gently lowered it to the floor.

"The back window," Mary was screeching. "I saw a shadow. Get out there and look, Pat. Get out there."

She came from her chair and knelt to take her father's head in her arms. She was weeping, and at the same time she was showing strength, Pat thought. She wrenched a revolver from the Gabe's belt and handed it over.

"Go, damn you, go!"

Pat automatically accepted the weapon. He ran through the kitchen and out into the rear of the lot. There was a shed, and he ducked, zigzagging, going around it. He pulled up short in the growing darkness. The ground was hard, there had been no rain, and he could see no footprints. He knelt, examining the earth at the place where the murderer must have been — there was no other cover, this had to be the spot. He saw it at once — an empty shell to match the one his father had shown him.

He picked up the empty metal hull and peered at it. There was something all wrong with this, he thought. He carried the shell back to where the kitchen light shone upon it. The same hammer mark, a trifle off-center, was plain to be seen.

He put the shell away and ran through the alley between Lin Chee's and the general store owned by the Gordons. Main Street was still empty. He crossed to Carmer's place. The saloon was deserted except for the proprietor and his barkeeper, Stremple. Carmer was leaning on the end of the long, curved bar. Stremple was polishing glasses. They were both dapper men. They had come to Scottsville together and could have been partners for all anyone knew, although Stremple always remained behind the mahogany, never asserting himself.

"Was there anyone in here or on the street — or any place you could see in the last half hour?" demanded Pat.

"Why, no. Everybody keeps out of sight since the fight the other night. I thought I heard a shot. Or what might have been a shot," Carmer said. "Did you hear it?"

"It was a shot," Pat said. "It killed my father."

Carmer came away from the bar, stricken. Stremple stopped wiping at a beer glass, leaning forward, peering at Pat in disbelief.

"Doc Gill. Did you call on Doc Gill?"

"Mary's with Pop," Pat said. "No use to call the doc. It got him in the heart."

"Then he wasn't imagining that someone tried to kill him. When Buster was shot, I mean," Carmer said. "The Lazy M men aren't home yet, are they?"

"They couldn't have driven the herd up here by now," Pat said. "Someone could have made the ride, though."

Carmer said, "It's hard to believe. Gabe was sure that it wasn't an Indian with a grudge. Do you agree?"

"I agree. Not an Indian," Pat said. "Excuse me."

He went out of the saloon. Now there were people: the Gordons; Jackson, the Wells Fargo man; Owens from the bank, Sheriff Masters and others. Old Dr. Gill was just entering Lin Chee's restaurant. Pat felt a great reluctance to go to his father. There was nothing in there but a shell — he would never hear the gruff, rasping voice again. He felt tremendous loss, emptiness. His life would not be the same from now on. Nothing would be the same for Mary or for him. They had inherited a ranch and a feud. Now there was murder, and neither he nor she was prepared.

He forced himself to go across the street toward the restaurant. He had a very unpleasant duty to perform. He had to ask Doc Gill to pry the bullet from the body of his father. Again, he thought there was something terribly wrong about the empty shells left at the scenes of the two shootings. No killer in his right mind would leave such telltale evidence. Of course, it would be impossible to identify the murder weapon, even with the slightly off-center hammer marking. Many of the new rifles were not precisely true, owing to hasty manufacturing methods. And almost everyone owned either a new Winchester or Remington.

Mary was rigidly standing against the wall looking down at her hands. There was a group around Dr. Gill. Pat went to his sister.

She held out her hands. "Blood, Papa's blood."

"You'd better get away from here. I'll take you to the hotel for tonight."

"No. I've got to stay with him."

"Please, Mary. I'll stay."

"You? You never stayed with him. You went away and left him, and now he's dead," she moaned.

Another girl came through the door. Behind her came Vic Carmer, unhurried and grave. The girl was small and fair, with a sprinkling of freckles across her little nose. She wore a summer dress, and she was beautiful, in the eyes of Pat Goodwin. Mary spied her and stiffened with rage.

"You, Linda McKay! How many of your killers are in town this evening? How many? Which one shot my father?"

Pat said, "Mary, quiet!"

It was Carmer who came to them. He nodded to Pat and stepped to Mary's side. He spoke in a voice so low that only Pat could hear him.

"Mary, please. Come to the hotel. Please, Mary."

She opened her mouth to scream, then closed it. Tears ran from her eyes and slipped slowly down her cheeks. She put out a hand, and Carmer took it. He led her to the door, through it and onto the street. Her head was bent. She wept but she went willingly as a child while the gambler spoke to her in a soothing, quiet tone.

Linda McKay said, "I'm sorry, Pat. I'm truly shocked and sorry."

"Yes. It's shocking and sad. Nothing's worth killing over. Thank you, Linda." He could not take his eyes from her even though she averted her face, biting her lip.

She said, "I know Father will be grieved. The feud — it seems so unimportant all of a sudden."

"It was for a fact," Pat said. "I hope your father will listen to reason now. I hope so."

A flicker of anxiety showed on her mobile features. "Did you — have you seen Father? I had word he was riding ahead of the herd and coming in this evening."

"I haven't seen anyone but Vic Carmer and the sheriff. And now all these people who were hiding because of the riot."

She said, "The riot? You mean the fight?"

"Pop thought it was serious."

"A fight in Carmer's saloon serious? I wanted to talk to your father about that. My men said they didn't even know what started it," she said, an edge of sharpness in her voice. Then she remembered and shook her head. "Not now, and I apologize. Later we can talk."

"I'd like to talk to you."

"Later," she said firmly. "When — when things are quieted down."

"There's just one thing."

"What is that?"

"I'm going to learn who killed my father before things can be quieted down," he told her. "In spite of the way I feel about you — everything — I'm going to find the killer."

She turned and walked out of the restaurant. His heart flipped over, but he went grimly to Doc Gill to make his request for the lead which had entered his father's body and taken his father's life.

As dusk fell on the outskirts of Scottsville, man and horse were both lathered with sweat. Scott McKay pulled up beside a tall thicket. "Who's there?"

Hunt stepped out, leading a horse as badly worn as McKay's. His right hand was held shoulder high.

"Peace, boss. Want to talk to you."

"I don't want to talk to you, Hunt."

The gunslinger said, "Light's bad, or you'd see what I got in my hand. Here."

McKay caught the package tossed to him. It was a wad of bills tied with a string.

"That's all I took from you, every dollar."

"What's this mean?" McKay was astounded and suspicious.

"Want my job back."

"I don't want you." He pocketed the money. "This will prevent my sending the law after you. But I don't need you any longer."

"You don't? Now I wonder why? Wonder

why you're comin' *from* town when you just rode in. Goin' in circles — that ain't like you, boss."

"I'm going to the ranch."

"But your daughter's in town to meet you."

"How do you know?"

"Why, I been around awhile. I came in just behind the stage. Near killed a horse makin' it. I was up on that hill, you know the one. Sorta watchin'."

"I see." He was trapped.

"They're makin' a big fuss over Gabe Goodwin gettin' shot, ain't they? Was he killed?"

"I don't know."

"Well, if they knew you or me was around at the time the gun was fired, we would be in a fix, wouldn't we?"

"I didn't kill him!"

"Uh-huh. I believe that, and you're the boss and all. But would anybody else believe it?"

"Did you shoot him, Hunt?"

"From that hill? I ain't that much with a rifle. I'm more of a short gun man, y' know."

"How do I know you were on the hill?"

"How do I know you didn't shoot Goodwin?" Hunt grinned. "Look, I gave you back the money. More than you pay me in a year. Don't you even want to know why?"

"All right. Why?"

"Because a certain son named Buchanan is headed this way wearin' the badge of a Ranger. I ain't never killed a Ranger. Figures a man has to start sometime."

"Buchanan? A Ranger? That's nonsense."

"Wait and see."

"But that's impossible."

"Seems like, only it ain't. You want to listen to a story? Hard to believe but true?"

McKay's shoulders drooped. "All right. I'll listen."

He heard Hunt out with growing, frightened belief. He sat on the tired horse awhile when the tale was ended. Then he spoke wearily, resignedly.

"All right, Hunt. You're hired."

"You won't be sorry."

They rode toward town together. Maybe he wouldn't be sorry, McKay thought, and maybe he would. Events were crowding him, and he was not as tough and strong as he had thought he was.

CHAPTER FOUR

Coming from the south and across country, Buchanan, with Coco in tow, circled the town and headed for the GG Ranch. It was his intention to talk with Pat Goodwin first, then to survey the field of action. They came to a wooden sign pointing the way in letters burned with a branding iron.

There was, as yet, no barbed wire. The graze which Gabe had taken for himself was huge, cattle spread across it in the tall grass. There were longhorns and Herefords brought in to improve the breed, and all seemed peaceful and prosperous.

"But where at are the herders?" Buchanan asked. "There's always a few Indians ready to cut out beef for eatin' purposes."

Coco said, "I dunno . . . You the Ranger man. I jest the deppity. I ain't even got no badge."

"I keep telling you that you're the secret agent. And it's about time we separated. Next time you see me — you don't know me. You never met me."

"You gonna wish you never met me.

Wait'll this is over. I make you sorry you ever met me."

"Yeah," Buchanan said. "You said that a few times."

"Wouldn't want you to forget it."

"I'll try not to forget it. Now remember, you're a prizefighter looking for a bout."

"Prizefightin's agin' the law in Texas."

"We've been all over that." Buchanan was patient. "You go into Carmer's saloon. You ask if there's any sports in town. Illegal fights draw the sports like they're flies. We'll get a line on who is who and why."

"Black man in a little bitty town — it ain't good."

"You're not a black man, you're a prizefighter."

Coco considered this. "Like a racehorse?"

"Figure it out for yourself. Anyway, you go in and do like I say. Remember, you're an undercover deputy."

"Okay. I do it. But I don't have to like it."

"That's right. Just do it." He watched the bulky man ride toward Scottsville. Coco was a good horseman. In fact, he was a pretty good all-around fellow to have with you, he thought. If it wasn't for his insistence on finishing their fisticuffs, he'd be a pleasure.

He followed the dirt road which led to the ranch house of the GG. There was no one in sight; he had not encountered a single human being that day. He began to wonder if everyone was engaged in rioting at Scottsville. If he had sent Coco into that sort of situation, he had done a great injustice. He touched Nightshade with his heel, and they went swiftly along the way. There were cottonwood trees and a winding path and then the house, a rambling frame building, L-shaped, with a sloping roof. He rode quickly to the rear where the kitchen must be located, knowing that if there were inhabitants present this would be the likely place.

The yard was deserted. Nobody answered his hail. There were horses standing hipshot in the corral but no riders. He yelled again, "Pat! Pat Goodwin!"

From behind him a shrill voice said, "Just hold your hands high and turn around stranger."

He obeyed, kneeing Nightshade so that horse and rider now faced the barn. He blinked. The man with the rifle was jockey-sized. He wore a hat with a brim too wide, and two six-guns were enormous on his hips. In his hands was a double-barreled shotgun which, if loaded with buckshot, could cut even a man Buchanan's size in half.

"I'm a friend of Pat's," he said.

"You're wearin' Ranger badge," the man said. "We got a message to look out for

Rangers hereabouts."

"Where's Pat?"

"You didn't come through town?"

"No, I wanted to see Pat first."

The man said, "If you hustle, you can maybe make the funeral."

"Funeral? Pat's funeral?"

The tiny man spat. "Naw. Gabe's funeral."

"Gabe was healthy enough in El Paso the other day."

"That was before somebody ventilated him." The little man did not seem overly concerned. "Everybody's at the buryin' ground."

"And who are you?"

"Me, I'm Ed Dungan. Somebody hadda stay in case McKay tried anything. And I'm just the one. You wanta pull your stake, or you wanta be tied up 'til Pat gets here?"

"I'd admire to see you tyin' me up — but I better get to town," Buchanan said. "See you later, Dungan."

"I hope not. I don't cotton to big ugly bruisers."

It did not seem in the interest of peace to reply. The small man held the shotgun. Buchanan pointed Nightshade for town and rode as swiftly as possible.

It was hard to believe that the rough, tough, violent Gabe Goodwin was dead, that they were actually burying him. He had been the kind of man, Buchanan thought, who lived until a ripe old age, giving everybody a fit until the end. He thought of his own position as a Ranger sent to quell a riotous town now involved in a shooting. Major Jones would expect results — the major never made allowances.

He was, he saw, coming to the slope which led to Scottsville too late for the services. Wagons, carriages and horsemen were going in the direction of town. Evidently, everyone in the county had turned out for the funeral. He rode in behind the last carriage and saw that Pat Goodwin was driving with a tall, dark girl at his side. That must be Mary Goodwin, Buchanan thought.

He saw McKay and some men in a bunch riding apart from the procession. He was surprised to see the Lazy M man, and immediately his mind began to run over certain inalienable facts. If Gabe had been "ventilated," McKay was certain to be suspect if he had been anywhere in the vicinity. The fact that he had ridden ahead of his recovered herd would be a factor against him . . . Unless there had been a shoot-out . . . But if there had been a showdown, McKay would not be present at the funeral, he would be forted up on his ranch northeastward of Scottsville . . . Buchanan knew it was bound to be complicated. Nothing had been simple since before he had joined the Lazy M on the ill-fated — for Buchanan — excursion into Mexico. All he had to show for his travail was a hundred and forty dollars — less actual expenses, the balance in his oilskin tote bag — and a growing headache. He was a man of peace, and who had ever heard of a peaceable Texas Ranger?

He reined in at the edge of town and watched the men drift to the saloon. It was a very small town indeed; it seemed to have just one of everything. There were the store to supply food and general merchandise, one bank, one livery stable, one restaurant and, marvel of marvels, only one saloon. That must be Vic Carmer's place, and Coco must already be inside attempting his masquerade as an eager fighter. Although, Buchanan added to himself, if anyone did want to stage a boxing match Coco would be ready and eager, so it wasn't a part difficult for him to play.

Pat Goodwin got out of the hired carriage at the hotel and handed down his sister. A tall, black-garbed man seemed to take over there while Pat drove the carriage to the stable. McKay and the Lazy M men rode out eastward, evidently for the home ranch. A man with a star on his shirt pocket went to the restaurant. Pat came back and joined him there.

When they had all dispersed, there was a girl left over. She had spoken to McKay from the veranda of the hotel. Now she remained there, as Mary and her dark-clothed friend went past her. The man spoke to her, but Mary flew into the hotel lobby.

Buchanan watched it all, then rode to the livery stable and put up Nightshade. The stableman, named Bondi, was a swarthy, crooked-legged fellow who seemed partially deaf. He eyed Buchanan's star and blinked, then confined himself to monosyllables, pretending not to hear questions.

He walked back toward the restaurant intending to have his talk with Pat. The girl on the hotel veranda lifted her skirt and came running across the street. She was so small he had to bend over to get a good look at her. Even as she spoke, he knew who she was: she was a softer and vastly prettier edition of her wiry, dark father.

"Mr. Ranger . . . I mean, you're Mr. Buchanan, aren't you?" Her voice was sharper, more distinct than the slurred speech of Texas, and he remembered that she had grown up in the north.

"Now, how did you know that?"

"I knew it." She compressed her lips, which were red without artifice and as shapely as an Indian warbow. She spoke quickly, "There was a telegram."

It seemed to him that she was not telling

the truth. No one in Scottsville had foreknowledge of his name, so far as he could figure. He said, "I don't need anyone to tell me you're Miss McKay."

It was her turn to be surprised. "I am Linda McKay."

"If your father was a beauty, he'd look like you."

She flushed. "That's what I want to talk to you about. My father. Some people are saying he either shot Mr. Goodwin or was responsible for it. And I want to tell you it is not true. I want you to know my father would never bushwhack anyone, not his worst enemy."

"The way I hear it, Gabe was his worst enemy."

"They were squabbling, that's true. Like children." She gestured with a tiny hand. "A lot of silliness."

"It didn't strike Pat as silly," Buchanan said. "Seemed to me he was bad hurt by it all. On account of you."

Now she was deeply pink. "That's part of it. Just because I'm not — not — not in love with Pat, he chose to think it was because of my father's fight with his father."

"Well," Buchanan said, "any man meetin' you would be glad to hear you're not in love. Does that mean you're not in love with any other man?"

"I certainly am not!"

"Now that's real nice. You goin' to be in town tonight?"

"I don't know what you mean."

"Oh, yes, you do. If you get any redder you're goin' to look like a sunset. A real lovely sunset," Buchanan said. "If you do stay over, I'd admire to take you to supper."

She smiled, and the color diminished to a natural shade. "We'd make an odd couple, wouldn't we?"

"I can always bend down to a lady," Buchanan said. "In this case, it's a pure pleasure."

She said, "I do want to talk about the feud. And the fight the other night. And my father."

"Six o'clock?"

She inclined her head. "I'll be expecting you."

She tripped back across the street. She had ankles like an antelope's, and she moved with an antelope's grace. He watched her go into the hotel. It would be a shame if her old man had killed Gabe, a real shame, Buchanan thought. He went on into the restaurant.

The hotel was actually a converted stage station. It was built of stone and strong, ancient timbers which had withstood many an Indian attack. The rooms were square and large, converging around a square in two ells. In one of them, with the door firmly closed, Mary Goodwin wept and clung to Vic Carmer.

He said, "Really, my dear, we shouldn't be here like this. It would cause talk, you know."

"Who cares?" she demanded, her great eyes filled with tears. "Who gives a damn? Not my brother. Not anyone in the world but you."

He gently pressed her down onto the only chair in the room and said dryly, "I believe your brother would care if he saw us now. In fact, I know he would. At the point of a gun. Aimed at me."

"He's a coward, a mule calf. He refuses to go after McKay. He's in love with that midget, that horrible daughter."

"She is not really horrible," Carmer said. "Now that your poor father is dead and buried, maybe you should make friends with the McKays and discontinue the feud."

"Make friends with the murderers of my father? Are you mad, Vic? Are you turning against me too?"

He said quickly, "Of course not. I'm with you always, my dear, you know that."

She jumped to her feet. She cried, "Then marry me! Take over the ranch with me. We'll wipe out Lazy M and own the plains."

She threw herself at him, and he held her, shivering a little, his face drawn and white. Her strong arms held tightly to him.

He said in his quiet voice, "My dear, you know we cannot marry so soon after your father's death. It would be wrong — everyone would be against us. We must think of your brother whether we like it or not. He isn't a man who can be tossed into a corner like an empty sack."

"He is . . . He is . . . He never loved my father . . . He was Mama's boy. He was always Mama's boy. We can handle him. I only need a strong man to back me up." She kissed him. "Oh, I love you. I want to marry you."

"Yes, darling, yes." He could always soothe her. He had learned her wild ways long since and had found that his voice, his poise, a certain tone could bring her down from her flights of fancy. "Let us be reasonable, for now. If we married we would have problems with our own men: the riders, your gunman Dungan. They have their own peculiar notions, these people. They think of me as a gambler and saloonkeeper, acceptable but not in your class. You are the rancher's daughter. They'll do anything for you — for us, they'd do nothing. Believe me, I know these men."

"We'll hire a new crew. Tougher, real gunslingers. I want Lazy M destroyed, you understand? I want it burned to the ground, I want them all dead! I want that girl disgraced and run out of the country!"

He again felt a chill, but he maintained his steady, even tone. "In time, darling, in time. You must be patient. Let me manage matters. Maybe your father's killer will be found, there'll be investigation . . ."

"By Fred Masters? That nincompoop?"

"Wait and see," he said. "The time is not ripe for a rash act. Trust me, will you, darling?"

He returned her kiss, holding her tightly, bending her at the waist, mastering her through her willingness, her eagerness. He felt her relax and knew he had won. He disengaged himself and smiled tenderly at her.

"Now I must slip out of here before anyone thinks to check on us."

"Later? Will I see you later?"

"It will be a busy time at the place," he said. "If I can get away. Just be quiet and think, darling. Just take it easy for now. You need rest and sleep."

"Nobody cares but you," she said. But she was docile as he opened the door, looked right and left, threw her a kiss and departed. She stretched herself on the bed and closed her eyes. She had a bad headache. They came oftener lately. Sometimes she scarcely remembered what she had said. She knew she was desolate at the loss of her father. She knew she was furious at

Pat. She knew she loved Vic Carmer. Other matters got mixed up in her mind very often.

But she would make it work. She would act. She would show them all that she was Gabe Goodwin's daughter . . .

Buchanan sat in the chair in which Gabe had been sitting when the shot came through the rear window. "Yeah. He would have seen anyone excepting behind that shed. He was looking, you said. He acted — worried. I'm no detective, but that's common sense. And he was going to tell you something about the bullet."

"I had Doc Gill get the bullet for me." Pat took out a wad of cotton and set it before Buchanan. "Doc says it . . . it struck a bone and you can't tell anything about it."

Buchanan looked at the little lead slug which had taken a man's life. The man had been seated in this spot. He had been alive, vital and engaged. He had been speaking, he was preparing to eat, he was a whole man. Then someone had fired this bit of metal into him and had ended his days on earth.

Through the rear window, he thought, and turned to stare. He could see the outline of the shed, the edge of it. He could see . . .

He swept both great arms. He knocked

Pat onto the floor. He sent the sheriff sprawling. He dove straight forward as if into a lake.

There was a bee whine and then a faint report. The window at the front of the restaurant splintered without crashing, showing a hole with striations extending from it. Buchanan rolled over and drove for the kitchen without coming to full height. He ran into Lin Chee, tripped and went headlong into the back door.

By the time he got to the shed, he realized he was unarmed. It was hard to break his habit of leaving his gunbelt in his bedroll. Still he lunged ahead, going around the shed to where the shooter had stood.

Pat was right, the ground was too hard. Someone was moving very fast around the rim of Scottsville. Buchanan cast around, east and west, then south. There were elders, willows and plenty of buffalo grass, but there were no signs worthy of note. He came to the livery stable separated from the restaurant by a wide alley. Bondi was in the yard with a pitchfork. Pat Goodwin came in from the street, his face pinched with rage.

Buchanan asked Bondi, "Has anyone come past here? Through here?"

"What? What you say?" The man cupped an ear.

"He couldn't hear a shot that distance

away," Pat said. "He couldn't hear anyone running through here. If he didn't see anyone, he wouldn't know if they did come through."

"Maybe he wouldn't say if he knew?"

"Maybe," Pat said helplessly. "How can you tell? He don't hear much, and he never says much. He lives alone and minds his business, is all I know about him."

Buchanan said, "Let's go back to that shed."

They walked the back way. This time they found it at the base of the foundation of the shed. It twinkled up at them, a brass shell. Buchanan picked it up and shook his head.

"Nobody's that dumb. This is some kind of a message."

"I agree with you," Pat said.

"Where's your sheriff? What about him?"

"When you knocked us down, he struck his skull," Pat said. "He's not real bright. He's a friend and honest enough but not smart, you know?"

Buchanan put the empty brass shell in his pocket. "You see about him, will you, Pat? I'm going over to the saloon. Want to talk, also listen . . . And Pat, I'm having supper with the McKay girl."

"Linda? You're havin' supper with her? How come?" Pat's eyes changed color. He was between anger and disbelief.

"To talk and to listen. It's the only way I

know. Some fast-movin' killer has got a plan. He got Gabe. He don't want a Ranger around nosin' into things. He moves like an Indian."

"Pop was real hard on Indians," Pat said. "He believed the only good ones were dead ones. He caught one rustlin' beef and hung him."

"Apache or Comanche?"

"Pop didn't ask," said Pat. "He was a hard man."

"What about your sister?"

Pat shook his head. "She's nearly *loco.* She and Pop were real close. And she thinks McKay is responsible for every bad thing that happens."

"You don't think so?"

"McKay's no bushwhacker."

"That's right. But he hires gunnies."

"So did Pop. I'm goin' to fire that miserable little Dungan first thing."

"Don't," Buchanan said. "You might need him."

Pat said, "I don't see why you're pesterin' Linda McKay. She can't know anything useful."

"Why, that's no task," Buchanan said cheerfully. "She's a right pretty little thing."

Pat glowered at him. "Now, don't you get fresh about Linda. I don't think you oughta bother her."

"I won't bother her any. You're mighty

tetchy about the gal, ain't you?"

"Never you mind." Pat was really huffy. "I'd better see about the sheriff."

He walked away without ceremony. Buchanan lifted one big shoulder and started for the saloon across the way. If the girl didn't love the boy, he thought, Pat should get down off his bandwagon. The sorriest sight in the world was a man chasing a woman who didn't want him. The best thing a friend could do would be to show him that he was out of it — clear the air, bring forth the truth.

Besides, the girl sure was as pert as an Appaloosa pony. Scarred as he was, he had known women to be attracted to him. Little women, in particular. Maybe it was his enormous size, the fact that they had to look up to him. He had pondered on it from time to time and finally decided that reasons didn't matter — so long as they liked him. He had seen something in the eyes of Linda McKay, and he was determined to find out what it meant.

The door to Carmer's place was wide open. From inside came a farrago of noise. It was the same way after all funerals, Buchanan reflected. Everything was solemn, quiet and respectful until the dirt was thrown onto the coffin, then all hell broke loose. It came from the great relief of the survivors, the thankfulness that it was some other person and not themselves. He paused on the threshold of the saloon.

He could identify most of the men through Pat's descriptions. He saw Coco at center bar, the object of everyone's attention. To the rear was the black-garbed, self-effacing man who had to be Vic Carmer. Behind the bar was Stremple. There was a man needed watching, Buchanan thought. There was another bartender, a huge figure as big as a house. Pat had mentioned him, a part-time horseshoer in a place where every ranch had its own smithy. His name was Oliver Green. His arms were bare above the elbow, and his muscles bulged like musk-melons. Just about every man in Scottsville was in the saloon. They were a scruffy lot except for the owner and a well-dressed man with muttonchop whiskers who sat at a table alone and who had to be the banker, Oswald Owens.

As Buchanan's tall shadow fell across the room, the noise diminished, running down-hill to a stop. Coco blinked and turned his back, muttering something about "doggone Rangers."

"Name's Buchanan. Don't let me interrupt anything." He walked slowly the length of the barroom, looking at each one of them, identifying them according to Pat Good-win's descriptions. He took his place along-side Carmer and said, "I'll have a beer."

The big blacksmith served him, beetle-browed, frowning. Desultory talk began on a low note. It seemed that they were dissembling, abandoning the subject under discussion when Buchanan had appeared.

"I'm Vic Carmer," the man in black said. "I suppose you want to talk about the tragedy."

"Want to go back a bit, Carmer," Buchanan said bluntly. "Had a riot here a few days ago. What started it?"

"Who knows?"

"Weren't you around when it happened?"

"No. My bartenders were in charge."

Buchanan turned to the big man. "You're Oliver Green?"

"What's it to you? I ain't done nothin'."

"You mean not ever? Or just lately?" Buchanan asked.

"Not never. And if I did would I be tellin' it to some big jasper with a tin badge?" Green thrust his heavy jaw forward as though daring Buchanan to punch at it.

"Polite barkeep you got there," said Buchanan to Carmer.

"Oliver, go to the other end of the bar, please." Carmer did not raise his voice. "Sorry, Ranger. There's little choice of help in Scottsville. It's a quiet little town."

"With a riot and a murder on its hands."

"True. Sadly true."

"Would your other barkeep know what

started the fight in here that night?"

"Stremple."

The dapper man came and put his hands on the bar and stared at Buchanan without emotion. "Lazy M and GG Ranch. That's your answer. I'd say Lazy M didn't start it."

"Then the GG men did?"

Carmer said, "They usually do fight. Fortunate Ed Dungan wasn't in it. Masters takes his guns when he comes to town, but he's been known to carry a hideout. Lazy M has a fellow called Hunt."

"I had the pleasure of meetin' them both," Buchanan said. "So the riot was just part of the range war."

Stremple said, "Well, Oliver there, he was coldcocked when the lights went out. That's why he's so mad. Then they got into the street, and somebody got a gun, and shots were fired. Sheriff got the wind up. Reckon he sent for you."

"Gabe Goodwin thought it was important. Gabe didn't scare all that easy when I knew him."

"I wouldn't know about that, Ranger."

Stremple was being more than cooperative, almost ingratiating. He didn't resemble that kind of customer to Buchanan. There was something between Carmer and Stremple, some communication: their eyes met, slid apart and met again. People like that abounded in the land, and they were to be watched; not that they were crooked or evil, but that they were dangerous to go up against. They worked together too well.

The banker, Oswald Owens, now rose and strolled to join them. He introduced himself and said, "Ranger, you came in here at an inopportune moment."

"That's what I thought I recognized," Buchanan said.

"You look like a man with sporting blood. As if you'd been in a few scraps yourself."

"I wasn't always a Ranger," Buchanan said truthfully.

"Well, you know how it is. Men get together." He coughed. "Even on such a sad occasion . . . one must go on, life must be maintained, relaxation helps."

"It sure does, now, don't it." Evidently, Coco had stirred up some monkeys.

"This Negro here, he claims to be a prizefighter. He offered to fight anybody in the world."

"You mean this man?" Buchanan stared at Coco. "Well, he's got the look of it."

"How do you stand on the ban against prizefighting, sir?" asked Owens. "And is it within your jurisdiction?"

Buchanan pretended to consider, quaffing his beer. "The way I see it, I was sent up here to stop a riot, find out why it happened. Ran into a murder, two murders. I'll be real busy. Seems to me this is a local affair, out of my hands, sort of."

"Good!" the banker said. Avarice shone around him like a halo. "Then let us proceed."

"Yeah," said Oliver Green from the end of the bar. "He wants a fight, I'll give him a fight."

The local talent cheered. The saloon came alive with their chatter. Coco shadowboxed in the center of a ring of jeering and cheering local gentry.

Vic Carmer said, "Harmless enough, I expect. There'll be a small purse for the winner. The town will enjoy betting."

"I'll bet a hundred dollars on the Negro," Owens said promptly. "Green is no professional, merely a strong dummy."

"I believe I'll accept that wager," Carmer said. "Have to back the local talent, you know."

"Done and done," Owens said. He went among the people, trying for more bets.

Buchanan said, "That man likes money."

"All bankers like money," Carmer observed. "Owens, rather more than most."

"What about your local law?"

Carmer said, "Masters won't interfere — unless McKay or . . . well, Pat Goodwin now, I suppose . . . unless the cattle people object."

"He takes orders from them?"

"They are the ruling factors hereabouts,"

Carmer said. "They spend the money that keeps Scottsville — and this place — alive. Barely alive. Without them — nothing."

"So it seems. No farmin' or minin' here?"

"You can't farm without fence." Carmer smiled gently. "Barbed wire hasn't come to Scottsville. The mines played out years ago. The diggings are still up there not too far from town. No, there's nothing around here but cattle and only two ranches."

"Two big ones."

"Yes."

"Big and rich."

"Of course." The saloonkeeper was closing down, removing himself from the conversation. "Excuse me, I think they need help in arranging this boxing bout."

Stremple brought a second beer, and Buchanan leaned his elbows on the bar, watching and listening. The banker was a greedy man willing to evade the letter of the law to make a dollar. Carmer was the sort of man who did not seem to belong in Scottsville, an educated sharper who could make a living anywhere far better than here. Stremple played bartender, but there was more to him than struck the casual observer.

From what he could gather amid the turmoil, everyone except Carmer and his bartenders wanted to bet on Coco. Either they were following the banker's belief that no amateur could whip a professional, or they had no confidence in Oliver Green. That worthy was scornful, proclaiming loudly that "no black nigger bum" could beat one side of him. Coco continued to shadowbox and tell everyone that he was the "the champeen," although he did not designate what he was the champion of. Buchanan was bemused and interested. There would be more excitement when the riders from GG and Lazy M came to town, he thought. A cowboy would always bet his best saddle on a sporting event.

He finished his beer, unobtrusively made his way out of Carmer's place and walked down to the hotel. A man named Basilio was behind the desk, a Basque whose wife and daughters were the entire staff. He was a round-headed smiling fellow, the most pleasant Buchanan had yet met in Scottsville.

"Mr. Ranger Buchanan, yes. I have a nice room for you. In the right wing, no? You have suitcase, something?"

"Just a bedroll. I'll bring it in later. Like to wash up now, though."

"Good. Maria!"

A small plump girl appeared, dimpling, curtsying. She took a key from her father and led the way down a hallway on the right side of the building. The room was high-ceilinged and cool. Another girl, almost identical to Maria, brought water. He gave them two bits, and they bowed all the way to the turn of the corridor. He went into the room and washed up. He would have to change before having supper with Linda McKay, but that would be two or three hours from now. It was not time enough for a ride to Lazy M, but he wanted time before talking with McKay. He also wanted some time with Coco Bean. This would have to be private, without the knowledge of anyone in town.

He sat down on the bed and thought about it. It occurred to him at that moment that he did not have to go through with all this. He had been shanghaied into the Rangers and sent to Scottsville to prevent a riot from spreading. He was not a policeman and did not know a thing about crime detection. Here he was acting like a Pinkerton, and his only experience had been when, by error, he had been harassed by detectives, Rangers, marshals or sheriffs. Scottsville had a local lawman who knew the people and the terrain. All Buchanan need do is resign by mail or telegram and depart for the Black Hills, he told himself. If he had a brain in his head, he would do just that.

Two small matters deterred him. First, someone had taken a shot at him, and he could never, peace-loving man that he was, quite accept such a deed without reprisal. Second, he felt himself involved with people: Pat Goodwin, Coco the fighter — and maybe Linda McKay. There were unanswered questions in his mind about Scott McKay. And he was intrigued by Vic Carmer, the man out of place in the millpond which was Scottsville, and his bartender Stremple, who seemed a bit more than a type who served drinks to cowhands.

He glanced down at his badge. It was a bit tarnished. He used his kerchief to polish it so that it shone like the evening star. Then he went out to survey the geography of Scottsville, with particular attention to the shed behind the Chinese restaurant.

CHAPTER FIVE

The Lazy M ranch was built, like the Scottsville Hotel, of stone and heavy timbers. It was not, however, of ancient origin. Scott McKay, a northerner, believed in strongly built houses. He had made of his home a veritable fortress. He sat in his office in the rear and stared moodily out at the bunkhouse. Hunt sat across from him, smoking a thin cheroot and smiling a thin smile.

"The herd will be in tomorrow," said McKay. "I'll want you to do some work. It looks bad to the other men if you don't turn to once in a while."

"You ready to let Buchanan know I'm back here?"

"It's none of his business."

"Right. But he's my business. You know the town's got you pegged for killing Gabe Goodwin."

"That's not true. Nobody has accused me of anything."

"Nobody's got enough brains to buck you — or Pat and Mary Goodwin — exceptin' that outsized fake Ranger."

"He's not a fake. I wired Major Jones. Buchanan was sworn in."

"Sure he was. And that black, too, he was sworn in too? What's he doin' up here?"

"I don't know and I don't care. The men are all excited about the fight between him and Green."

"How come he was in jail with me and Buchanan and now he's up here? Last time I saw him he was goin' around and around with Buchanan. Now they act like strangers. There's somethin' goin' on, boss, and don't you forget it."

"I wish you'd stay out of town for a while."

"It's none of their business. You said it just now. Nobody's seen me yet. Just so you square me with Obie and Madigan and Bender before I have to shoot 'em, everything will be all right with me. Of course I could dry-gulch Buchanan, but that ain't my way. I want a showdown when things is right, and I'm goin' to get it."

"You're goin' to a lot of trouble just to shoot out with a man."

"It's my way," said Hunt stubbornly. "Besides, I'm plumb nosy. I'd like to know who did kill Gabe Goodwin."

"So would I."

Hunt grinned. "You sure you don't know? Or can't guess?"

"If I knew I'd be telling the law. Masters

and Buchanan. You think I want them suspicionin' me?"

"So we give 'em something to think about. If we could get rid of Buchanan, the local sheriff would be easy. You oughta move onto the GG pretty soon, boss."

"Move onto it? I intend talking with Pat. Maybe we can fix it so we both get along."

"Not while the gal's alive," said Hunt. "You know that as good as I do. The gal hates your guts and hates Miss Linda's guts and hates every man on the Lazy M. And I believe she's *loco*."

Scott McKay had no answer. In two days, his point of view had been rudely shoved this way and that until he did not know where he stood, what he believed, or what he intended. He wished he had not rehired Hunt; he wished he had never seen the man. He was frightened that his own daughter believed him somehow guilty of Gabe's murder. He wished she would come back to the ranch and lend him support. He felt his strength oozing from him. He felt Hunt was moving in far too close, taking too much upon himself, butting into matters which were not his concern.

He had always considered himself the leader; he had always been a successful, confident man. Gabe Goodwin's bluster had not frightened him; he had thought of the owner of GG Ranch as an old fuddy-duddy who had run out his string and was due to retire. Pat Goodwin had been no threat. In the end, McKay had known, all the high plain would be overrun with the Lazy M brand.

Now it was murder. He had seen men killed and had banged a rustler himself up in Montana. But cold-blooded murder was another matter. The aura of it stank, the shadow of it hung over everyone on the high plain.

And there was Buchanan. Why was his daughter being seen with the huge, enigmatic man wearing, incongruously, the badge of the Texas Rangers? Was she giving information? Was it possible she was falling in love with this wanderer who had been dead broke when McKay picked him up for the excursion into Mexico?

Hunt said, "Your mind wanderin', boss?" You got to think things out. You got to make a move."

McKay's perplexity turned to anger. "Get out of here, Hunt. Just get out. Find something to do. And stay away from town."

"Why, boss, you wouldn't know what's goin' on in town if it wasn't for me. Remember, I got a connection. I get the news."

"Just get out."

Hunt said shrewdly, "I know what's eatin' you. Nobody likes a bushwhacker. You'd rather have Gabe alive than dead the way he died. Okay. But think about what comes next. You got to do somethin'."

He lounged out. His attitude was that of a man who knew precisely what he was doing. This was another worry to Scott McKay. He knew he could not trust Hunt any further than he could throw his prize bull. He slumped in his chair, a comfortable throne from which only a few weeks ago he could dictate the affairs of Lazy M with confidence.

Buchanan walked to the stable and waved at Bondi, a man always busy at one chore or another. He lifted his saddle down from the peg and called to Nightshade. Bondi kept the horse curried, combed and well fed. There was a whinny of recognition, and then there was a low voice.

"Mr. Buchanan."

"Yes, it's me." He slowly began to adjust the cinch.

Coco's head protruded from the loft above. There were wisps of hay in his hair. He had been sleeping up there and, supposedly, training around the stable in preparation for the big fight.

"Fo' God, Mr. Buchanan, we's in trouble."

"You don't say."

"I sho do say. You know what they gonna make me do?"

"I could make a guess."

"You could?" Coco was amazed.

"With all that money on you and the smart ones takin' it, I would say they're askin' you to lay down. Dive. Lose."

"How you know that, Mr. Buchanan?"

"They showed you a .45 and promised you'd be dead if you win the fight. Correct?"

"That's just the way it was."

"And who made this threat?"

"That's what I don't know."

"What do you mean you don't know. You lyin' to me?"

"Mr. Buchanan, I was plumb fast asleep. It's dark up here at night. First thing I knows there is a cold, round somethin' in my ear. Somebody tellin' me to shut my mouth. Even if I yell, you know Bondi can't hear. Besides which, I am somewhat scared."

"Scared? You? I thought you were never scared."

"In daylight I ain't scared. At night it's different. Black night, a voice whisperin' at me. Tellin' me what'll happen to me if I win the fight."

"I see." He thought for a moment. Then he said, "We'll see about that when the fight takes place. Okay?"

"See about it? They'll have guns all over the place. What can we do 'bout it?"

"Have some guns of our own."

"But I'm up there all alone."

"Don't fret. You set up the old fight store for them. Not your fault. It's a swindle, it can be handled."

"I got an idea, Mr. Buchanan."

"Okay, let's hear it."

"You such a good fighter. Whyn't you box this blacksmith feller?"

"I'm a Texas Ranger, Coco. It wouldn't be right."

"But I'm a deppity Ranger."

"Sure, but nobody knows that." Buchanan backed the black horse out of the stall and reached for his bridle. "Just don't fret. It'll all work out."

Coco said plaintively, "I ain't scared. But I jest can't help bein' a bit nervish, Mr. Buchanan."

"No Ranger is ever nervous, Coco," Buchanan said severely. "Train hard. Be ready."

He mounted Nightshade and rode out. It had to be Stremple, he thought. He could not see Carmer climbing into a hayloft to make a threat. It would be Carmer's scheme, but the bartender would work it out. It was a con, and Buchanan had seen all the cons: the big store, the soap sellers, every known chicanery of the nimble-witted. Most of the loose money would be bet on the professional, Coco. The smart ones would clean up if Green won.

Problems had begun to mount. He rode

out westward toward the GG Ranch. He had to have a talk with Pat, and he had yet to meet Mary Goodwin. He had heard a lot about Gabe's militant daughter, but she had not been available for questioning. Fred Masters had warned him that he would be going against a female cougar with no chance of learning anything. This business of detective work was proving the most difficult problem Buchanan had ever attacked. He had not the slightest notion as to who had killed Buster the cook and Gabe Goodwin.

He did surmise that the empty cartridges left at the scene were supposed to be misleading clues. Gabe's last words as reported by Pat indicated the old rancher had known this. If true, this only proved that the killer had a devious mind and was much smarter than Buchanan liked to believe.

Last night, he had received a telegram from Major Jones demanding a report. Today he would have to comply. He would write it all down and send it back by the daily stage. He began to compose it in his mind.

It would not come clear. There were too many cross angles. Tomorrow or next day, the herd would be coming to Lazy M. Then he would go out there and see what he could learn. Perhaps he should not make the report until that time.

The road was clear, and the skies were mottled by cloud formations, the mountain peaks decorated with them. It was fine country, the high plains. He had always enjoyed a stay there — until now.

He thought of Linda McKay. He had taken her to supper twice and had sat upon the hotel veranda talking with her until quite late at night. They had discussed a hundred topics — and he had learned almost nothing about anything. He only knew that she loved and trusted her father and that she was afraid of and distrusted Mary Goodwin. He could have guessed that much without seeing the girl. But it was certainly a lot more fun to be with her. They got along as if they had known each other for years; there was a bond between them which both had recognized on first meeting.

He turned up the path he had traveled before. There was a new sign, hastily lettered: "NO TRESPASSING UNLESS YOU WANT TO GET SHOT." He blinked at it — GG Ranch was at war, as Linda McKay had prophesied sadly the previous evening. He rode around the grove of trees and called out in self-defense.

"It's me, Buchanan. Don't shoot."

Pat came out on the porch of the frame house. His sister was close behind him. Buchanan dismounted, calling a cheery greeting.

Dungan, the diminutive gunman, stepped from the trees and shoved a Colt's revolver into Buchanan's ribs. "You want this one kilt or run off?" he shrilled.

Pat said coldly, "Just run off. We have nothing to say to you, Buchanan."

As usual, Buchanan was not wearing his revolver. He looked at Pat and the girl. "But I've got to talk to you. Better call off your watch puppy."

"Can't I kill him?" Dungan begged. The top of his sombrero reached just to Buchanan's waistline.

"If he insists," Mary Goodwin cried. "He saw the sign. He's warned."

"No," Pat said. "He's a Ranger. You don't kill Rangers. They send a troop after you."

"He's a fake Ranger," she said. "He consorts with the McKays."

Buchanan said, "Oh, come on, now. I'm gettin' weary of all this caterwaulin'."

He made a sudden move. He slapped with both hands. Dungan's wrist was caught between. The Colt's flew a dozen feet away. He picked Dungan up by a shoulder and plucked the second gun from the holster. He carried the little man kicking and screaming up into the porch.

He said, "Honest now, this is somewhat ridiculous. Your papa got killed, and I'm tryin' to find out who did it and who took a shot at me. To say nothin' of your cook.

I can't be pestered by midgets nor anybody else."

He put the little man down and pointed a finger at him. "You as much as move," he continued, "and I'll take away your boots and your pants and stake you out for the chickens to nibble at."

The little gunslinger's hat had fallen off. He had a shock of wiry hair which grew down low on his forehead. His eyes were gimlets probing at Buchanan. "Now I will kill you. I promise. I swear it. I'll kill you, Buchanan."

"Everybody's goin' to kill me. Or beat on me. Or somethin'," Buchanan said in a discouraged voice. "Nobody wants to set down and talk things over. How'm I ever goin' to get anyplace if people act like this?"

"Pat, are you going to allow this? Are you going to stand for this bully coming here and acting this way?"

"Now, ma'am," Buchanan said, "I ain't really actin' up. All I want is to talk a little about what's been happening and the people around Scottsville and how we're goin' to find out who's been killin' from ambush. Way I see it, there ain't too many to suspect."

"Just the entire Lazy M crowd," she said. Her great eyes were burning. "If you want to do something arrest them. Take them away before we start dealing out justice."

Buchanan looked at Pat. "You start a war, and the Rangers will be here pronto. You know that better'n me."

"I know. I don't intend to start it," Pat said. He was sullen and unfriendly. "We're waiting for them to begin. I know they will."

"Gutless," Mary Goodwin said. "My brother hasn't got the nerve to carry slop to the hogs."

"I'll kill 'em," Dungan snarled. "Lemme take some boys over there. Let this — dirty — 'scuse me, Miss Mary — this here Ranger try and stop me."

Buchanan said, "Folks, there's no reason to believe McKay nor any of his people shot your cook or your father — or took a shot at me."

"They could have done it," Mary insisted.

"So could a lot of other people. There's another bunch works together around here," Buchanan said. "I ain't accusin' anyone. But Vic Carmer and his bartenders and a couple barflies and such . . ."

Mary Goodwin stamped her foot. "Don't you dare! Don't you dare put your filthy tongue on the man I'm going to marry!"

Buchanan stared at her in utter disbelief. "Marry? You're going to marry Vic Carmer?"

"You'd better believe it! I'm marrying a man who will take hold of things. Who'll avenge my father!"

"Is this true!" Buchanan asked Pat.

"She's free, white and twenty-one." There was no fire in Pat. He was withdrawn and disinterested.

Buchanan said, "Well, I swan."

"Oh, don't you start anything, don't you argue with me," the girl cried. "You've been hanging around that milk-fed Linda. You've made Pat unhappy, now you're trying it on me. I'm not Pat, and don't you ever forget it. I'm my father's daughter. I'm a fighter and a hater."

"Yes, ma'am, I can see that." He watched the midget gunfighter hang on every word uttered by Mary Goodwin. He saw the adoration in Dungan's eyes. Things were complicated in the Scottsville country. There was nothing to be gained here at the GG Ranch, he felt. "Well, okay. I'm makin' a report to Major Jones this evenin'. Have to tell him you're on the prod. Sorry about everything, folks. Real sorry. This is a tough spot for a peace-lovin' fella, believe me."

He went back to where Nightshade was grazing on the lawn, picked up the reins and rode out, not looking back. When he was out of their line of vision, he turned north and rode across a high pasture to the foothills. He had learned something — nothing helpful, but something — he thought. The day was lovely, the country beautiful, the clouds playfully changing shapes so that they resembled half the animals in a zoo, but the people of whom he thought were not so lovely.

Now the Goodwins, without the strong authority of Gabe, were unhappy and unsteady. Pat had the same old trouble, which had sent him away before: he was in love and Linda McKay was not. Mary certainly seemed one who was not responsible, and her announced marriage was a sure sign that this was so. Carmer was a handsome, well-educated, well-mannered individual, but he was of a certain stamp which Buchanan recognized as beyond the pale. The gambler did not belong among decent, industrious people. He was a parasite, a wolf on the edge of the herd waiting to cut down a cripple. His man Stremple was the same, a cut below Carmer in outward appearance, but a brother under the skin. As Buchanan's father in East Texas had always said, "They ain't our kind of folks."

He rode higher into the foothills. He had the outdoorsman's knack of being able to glance over terrain and never forget the outlines of the countryside. He wanted to know as much as possible about the land around Scottsville in case there was need, either in being chased or in pursuing a fugitive. He was skylined when he saw the man with field glasses, and he promptly dropped Nightshade behind a rocky prominence and dismounted. He took his rifle and crawled to a better point of vantage.

The man's horse was beneath a scrub oak, reins trailing. The glasses were trained on a herd of GG cattle, which were lazily browsing in a pasture of belly-high grass. There were two cowboys sleepily tending the herd. The man had a rifle within arm's length. It seemed to Buchanan that he was estimating the range between him and the herders.

Buchanan did some lightning calculation of his own. It added up to instant action. He did not take the time to go for his own rifle. He went downhill straight as a string, moving with all the speed of which his bulk was capable. The man with the field glasses heard him coming like an avalanche and made a grab for his gun. Buchanan leaped the last twelve feet and landed on the man's back. They rolled together for a moment or so, and then the man stretched out with his eyes wide and his breath gone. Buchanan took his revolver away and said, "Well, now, this is a surprise. How've you been, Hunt?"

Hunt managed to blurt, "Lucky again, you bastard!"

"Not me," Buchanan said. "You're the lucky one."

"Ha!" Hunt was trying to regain breath.

"Figure it out. Suppose you did get to kill one of those men down there. I would've had to cut you down *pronto*."

"I wasn't about to take a shot at anybody," Hunt said. "You're the only one I want to get."

"We know all about that. Well, we better go in. They have a nice jail in town."

"You got no reason to arrest me."

"How about you're wanted in El Paso?"

"You was in that as much as me."

"But I'm wearin' the badge," Buchanan said. "Supposin' we send a telegram to Major Jones about it?"

"Buchanan, killin' you once just ain't enough."

"Yeah. Well, reckon you're first in line. There's a whole heap of you nowadays, around and about."

He took Hunt's revolver and put him on his horse. He whistled to Nightshade to come down. He mounted and headed for Scottsville with Hunt riding ahead. It was his first arrest as a lawman, but he wasn't too set up about it. Hunt could have been in town when Gabe was shot — but not when Buster the cook had been killed. It was time to see McKay and have a long confab. Nothing was clear — everything was muddy as the Rio Grande at flood time.

CHAPTER SIX

Hunt, looking rather forlorn without his guns and much skinnier, gazed at the empty cells around him. "I got my choice, huh?"

"Take any one," Buchanan said. "The hoosegow is all yours."

"It's a pretty strong old building," Hunt said. He squinted at Sheriff Masters. "You better get you a few deputies."

"No need for 'em. Town won't pay, the county neither." Masters was always somewhat worried.

"You'll need 'em," Hunt said dully. "If Lazy M don't side with me — then the GG bunch'll be after me. For hangin'."

"Oh, come on," Buchanan said, "you ain't all that important hereabouts."

"Not me personal," Hunt agreed. "It's the times, the way things are."

He went into an ample cell and closed the door behind him. He tested the cot and grunted, easing his bones down on it, stretching full length, tipping his hat over his eyes. "Call me when the shootin' starts. I need some catch-up sleep."

Buchanan followed the sheriff out into the office. Masters sat down behind his desk and took out an official-looking form.

"What's the charge against Hunt?" he asked.

"Common nuisance?"

"I can't hold a man on that charge."

"Uncommon nuisance?" Buchanan suggested.

"Now, you got to remember, I was a friend of Gabe's, but I won't hold a Lazy M man, even a gunny, unless he's charged right and proper," the sheriff said.

Buchanan reflected. "Well, I can't say about the right and legal part. But Hunt escaped jail in El Paso. Maybe Major Jones wants him. You just hold onto him until I can get a message to the Rangers."

Masters brightened. "That'll do it. You got it. I can hold him pendin' an answer from the major."

"Meantime, I'll try and get out to Lazy M. Might turn off trouble with a little talk."

Worry lines appeared again across Master's brow. "The herd's in from Mexico. McKay's got his crew around him. Hunt's the bad man — but they're all tough."

"Everybody's tough in this country," Buchanan said. "Leastways, that's the way they come at you."

"Do you think I oughta swear in a deputy, like Hunt said?"

"Who, for instance?"

Masters nodded. "The crop ain't good in this town. Reckon I'll just have to ride it out."

"Reckon you will." Buchanan regarded the sheriff. "I wouldn't want anything to happen to my prisoner. Kind of keep a close eye on him, huh? I'll be back directly I attend to other business."

He unhitched Nightshade and walked down the street, big man and big horse. People regarded him solemnly, in a fashion to which he was not accustomed. It was the badge, he thought. He had been blackmailed into wearing it, and now it was taking on a luster which in his simple soul was not altogether unpleasant. He had arrested his first man and was about to make a report on it. He felt reasonably like a Texas Ranger.

He walked past the bank and the saloon owned by Carmer. It occurred to him that Lin Chee's restaurant and laundry were directly opposite the saloon. The wide shot which had been intended to kill him must have passed through the window and directly to Carmer's place. He tied up Nightshade, walked back and spied out a line to the chair in which Gabe had met his death. He turned and peered at the frame of the saloon.

There was a smudge in the new paint. He went closer. There was no bullet hole, just the spot where putty had been thumbed and painted over. Carmer sure was a neat man, he thought. Everything was spic and span and kept that way.

He went on to the Wells Fargo office, laboriously scratched out his report to Major Jones and gave it to Jackson. The agent and telegrapher wore an eyeshade — Buchanan had never seen one who didn't — and had a vaguely superior air, also peculiar to these strange individuals.

"That'll be a dollar," Jackson said. He was young, and there was something about him Buchanan didn't cotton to, an air of stuffiness.

"Send it collect," he said, showing his badge.

Jackson sniffed as if he had smelled something bad and replied, "If it's not accepted, you'll have to pay."

"Send it," Buchanan said without emphasis.

Jackson flinched but muttered, "Texas Rangers cut no ice up here, y' know."

"We don't? Then let it be said Buchanan can cut his own ice. You got any objections personal, like?"

Jackson said, "Uh — well, no."

Buchanan went out and mounted Nightshade. The policeman wasn't always respected, he ruminated. You had to take the bitter with the better. Jackson did not like

Rangers — it was something to file away in his memory. Jackson had been busy making bets, he knew, backing Oliver Green. It would bear some thinking on.

There was plenty to think about riding the eastward trail to the Lazy M Ranch. The coming nuptials of Mary Goodwin and Vic Carmer was one thing. It seemed an odd arrangement. No question that the gal was all for it — and Carmer would be at least making an attempt to marry into a position he could never achieve any other way.

But Pat's listless reaction, that was bad. It left Mary, Carmer and the midget Dungan in charge to start the fight with McKay. Buchanan had no desire to take sides, and the Goodwins were old acquaintances and all that, but he had to talk with McKay in order to stave off future problems. While Buchanan tried to reason with McKay, Hunt could rest on ice for a while.

He overtook a carriage. Linda McKay was on her way home, driving a fine chestnut horse. He rode up alongside, and she smiled across at him, reining in. He touched his hat.

"Howdy, Miss Linda. Nice day for a drive."

"Glad to see you, Tom. Father sent for me — I didn't have time to find you and tell you. It's been an exciting day. A wedding is in prospect."

"I heard."

"How did Pat take it?" she asked directly.

"Kinda strange. Like he didn't seem to care much about anything."

The tiny girl frowned. "If he had gumption . . ." She broke off and dimpled. "Father is worried about you and me."

Buchanan sat tall in the saddle. "Now that's the proudest thing I've heard since I came to Scottsville. You mean he's got cause?"

"You, Tom, are a fraud," she told him.

"Who, me? I'm just a big, handsome, devil-may-care *caballero*."

She said, "Pooh!"

"Pooh?"

"You've never once even tried to kiss me."

He reeled a little but recovered. "I held your hand in Lin Chee's. Although the smell of laundry soap don't do much for a spoonin' couple, I must admit."

"Spoonin'? When do we start?"

Gamely, he said, "Directly I have time to turn around. Been so much goin' on, I just plain haven't had the time."

"It's the desire that counts," she said. She grinned at him in the impish manner which so delighted him and chirruped to the horse.

As the carriage moved ahead, he pulled close alongside and leaned over. "Seems to me you're a bit feisty today. Could it be that you're thinkin' you mighta been Mrs. Vic

Carmer? If you played your cards right?"

Her hand flashed to the buggy whip in its socket, her eyes blazed. "You . . . damn you, Tom Buchanan!"

"Them that teases has got to be ready to take some teasin' back," he said. "Seems like you're mighty upset over a joke."

The horse walked slowly along, Buchanan holding Nightshade in as silence fell. The girl stared straight ahead.

Finally she said, "I'm not posing as a goody-goody, hoity-toity one. When Vic — when he first came to town, he was very attentive. And it made Pat jealous . . . and the way it was going with Pat and me . . . I did ride out with Vic. And he was a perfect gentleman."

"You sure don't get much of that spoonin' you talk about, do you?" Buchanan grinned.

Now she did laugh. "You're the limit. You're the absolute, unmitigated limit. Now let's get going home before some cowboy sees us and tells tales."

"A lot he'd have to tell," Buchanan said, but he followed along slowly behind her and up the side path to the Lazy M Ranch home buildings.

McKay was on the porch, staring. Madigan or Bender — he never could tell them apart — was nearby at the corral, fussing with a lariat. Obie Deal's square bulk was at the edge of the house. No doubt there were other Lazy M hands out of view — someone had indeed carried a tale.

Bender — or Madigan — came to the head of the chestnut and took hold of the bridle. Now Buchanan saw several more of the riders scattered about. They should have been attending cattle, he knew.

Scott McKay said with all of his old feistiness, "Linda, get down from that rig and into the house."

She came over the wheel with a flashing display of fine ankle and shapely calf. She said, "Don't you talk to me like that, father."

"Galivantin' around with this big saddle bum. Making a scandal of yourself in the land!"

She said, "You're crazy. Tom has been a big help to me and a perfect gentleman."

"Tom, is it? He's Buchanan, and he's a drifter and a fake Ranger." McKay swung around. "And if you light down on Lazy M land, you can forget that badge."

Buchanan swung a long leg and came down to earth. He said mildly, "Now, McKay, just slow it a bit. I came out here to warn you of trouble."

"You came right into trouble!" McKay shouted. "Nobody trifles with my daughter without getting something in return. Grab her." He pointed to his daughter and Madigan — or Bender — enveloped her as she ran to get between Buchanan and the Lazy M men.

Buchanan said, "Now is that any way to treat a lady? Looks like she's better off in my company."

Obie Deal and three other riders now began closing in. Obie was a tough citizen, and the others looked more like rough-and-tumble people than gunslingers, proving that McKay had planned pretty well, Buchanan thought. Linda struggled while McKay waved his men on.

Only Obie was willing. The others circled for a moment, but the foreman charged. He had big, hard fists, which he slung as though they were at the end of two busy flails. Buchanan sighed. Then he took two punches that hurt.

He hit Obie but not as hard as he could, because he respected the loyal, honest man. Obie went headlong to where Madigan — or Bender — was having trouble with Linda. The three of them staggered into Bender — or Madigan — which sent the chestnut to rearing, kicking and neighing.

The other three men came from various directions. Buchanan dealt with them without favor. He stepped to the right and knocked down the first. He stepped to the left and knocked down the second. He moved backward and knocked down the third. He looked reproachfully at McKay, who was skipping up and down in rage and frustration.

"Now look what you've done," Buchanan said. "You got your people here all messed up."

McKay dove for the porch and came up with a shotgun in his hands, all reason departed. "I'll kill you myself!"

Linda came with skirts tucked up. She rammed into her father. He sat down on the porch. There was a loud explosion as the shotgun went off.

Everyone froze where he was. Buchanan had forgotten he was still wearing his six-shooter. He now produced it and held it at his side.

McKay was babbling, "Linda, baby, are you all right? Oh my god, what have I done? Say you're all right, baby."

Linda disentangled herself and said, "The porch roof will leak from now on. Nobody around here can fix a roof."

"Oh, thank goodness, thank goodness," said McKay. He sat on the steps, head in his hands. "You men go away. Go take care of the ranch. Keep a watch for GG riders. Check on Hunt — that son will get us all into trouble yet."

Buchanan said, "You're right. But it won't be exactly his fault this time. I got him in jail."

"You arrested Hunt?"

The riders were hauling themselves to their feet, eyeing Buchanan, not altogether sure what had struck them. Now they backed away and one by one went about their business. Both Madigan and Bender took charge of the chestnut and the carriage. McKay sat, his spirit diminished, on the steps alongside his daughter.

Buchanan said, "He was over on GG land. And he's wanted in El Paso. Is it true he's still workin' for you?"

"Yes. He's working for me."

"Then I got to be scared of what Mary Goodwin will do. She thinks one of you killed her father."

"I know. That's the real reason I hired Hunt back."

"Hired him back?"

"You wouldn't know about that." McKay didn't offer to explain.

"Well, about Gabe, now."

"I didn't kill him," McKay said. "Hunt didn't kill him. No Lazy M person killed him."

Linda said, "I'm about sure of that by now."

"About sure?" Her father looked at her with dismay. "You're not real sure?"

"Why should anyone else want to kill Gabe Goodwin?"

"Lots of reasons," Buchanan said. "He hanged an Indian. He had a mean mouth.

He rode hard over anybody stood in his way. Thing is — he was bushwhacked."

"Yes. Murdered," McKay said. "I'm no murderer, Buchanan. And I don't believe Hunt is, either."

"I never said you were, neither of you. But you were up here ahead of the herd."

"Yes."

"Both of you."

"Yes."

"And you didn't see anything suspicious?"

"We didn't see each other. Hunt says he was on the hill behind Carmer's saloon, too far away to hit anything with a rifle — he's not much of a rifleman. I wasn't nearby, only heard the shot."

"You heard it pretty plain?"

"Well, yes. But — you know. Guns go off in this country."

"Up north they go off, too, don't they?"

"Well, sure, I meant in the West."

"You know gun sounds, one from another?"

"Well . . . no. I'm no expert."

"Okay. But how about the new rifles? The way they sound?"

"Oh. You mean sharp like. Not so booming."

"Right."

McKay considered. "I couldn't swear to it. But there was kind of a booming sound to the shot. It echoed around against the foothills."

Buchanan said, "Same way I felt when they took a shot at me the other day."

"At you? Why?"

"Maybe they were shooting at Pat Goodwin," Buchanan said. "I've thought on that."

"Yes," Linda said. "That would make it look as if Lazy M wanted to wipe out the Goodwins."

"And leave Mary alive?" Buchanan asked. "Whoever would try it — they don't know Mary Goodwin."

"He's right," Linda said. "Mary is the fighter. Pat — he just isn't. He hasn't got it in him."

Buchanan said, "You might just be wrong there, gal. Anyway, I wanted to ask some questions, let you know about Hunt. There'll be a crowd in town for the prizefight — you might figure. Fred Masters ain't what you might call a real tough man. A nice man, but kinda nervish. If you and your men come in, I'd appreciate if you'd lay kind of low. This bein' a lawman is new to me. Anything you can think of, let me know."

McKay said, "Buchanan, I apologize."

"For what?"

"Suspicioning you. Turning my men on you. Calling you a fake . . . everything."

"Why, that's all right," Buchanan said. "Hope I didn't hurt anybody. Tried not to. See you later."

Linda McKay said, "Haven't you forgotten something?"

"Huh?"

She perched on the top step and leaned forward, her head barely on a level with Buchanan's. "Just so Father won't think he had some grounds . . ." She pursed her lips.

"Linda!" her father cried.

Buchanan kissed her gently. "The first time — I sure hope not the last."

He went to Nightshade and mounted to the tune of McKay's shocked objections to his daughter's forward behavior. Now he had a lot more to think on.

Vic Carmer sat in the small office behind his saloon, to which very few people had ever been admitted. He was cleaning his fingernails with a tiny pocketknife; he had always been finicky about his nails and his hands. He thought about Mary Goodwin. He sighed deeply.

He had always been a man of large ambitions. Unfortunately, his talents had early been directed in the path of chicanery. Orphaned while in school, he had been left in custody of his uncle, Horatio Carmer, a man of many talents, none of which were honest. Uncle Horace shied away from work.

Well, Uncle Horace would work himself half to death, but it was always toward a dishonest end. The early West had been settled by earthy, simple folk, and Horace and his breed, the confidence men, had seized upon the situation to trim the suckers by every known crooked game. Thus, Vic had learned about the fight store when he was a stripling.

The coming of Coco Bean had proven too much temptation for him to resist. Oliver Green was the perfect "local" strong boy, being neither local nor particularly strong in the head, just bright enough to follow orders. Banker Owens had walked right into the play with his avaricious big mouth. It may have been a mistake, Carmer reflected, but Uncle Horace could never have passed up the chance.

Uncle Horace would never have passed up Mary Goodwin either, but his object would be only to cash in fast and vanish. In fact, Horace had come to an untimely end trying just such a caper with one Widow Brown. The lady had caught him decamping with her ready money and had blasted him in the seat of his pants with buckshot, bringing a painful death to the victim and providing Vic Carmer with a lesson not to be forgotten.

"No," he muttered. "If I go through with it I have to turn rancher and live here. I have to take Lazy M over. I could be a very rich man in a few years with Stremple handling the saloon and the town. But . . . can I handle her? Can anyone handle her?"

There was no present answer. There was a rhythmic tap on the door, and he bade Stremple enter. The bartender sat down and leaned back. Carmer reached for a bottle of ancient fine bourbon and poured two glasses, sparingly, since neither he nor his men were hard drinkers.

Stremple said, "That big dumb Buchanan just rode in. He was out to Lazy M."

"Not dumb," Carmer corrected his partner. "Slow and clumsy in a way, but not stupid — not Buchanan."

"He's annoying," Stremple insisted. "And he's no real copper. He couldn't figure out two plus two unless it was writ on the wall for him."

Carmer folded his little knife and placed it in his curiously designed belt, the buckle of which held a convenient over-and-under derringer deadly as a cannon at short range. He said, "Stremple, you will never understand the constabulary. Contrary to belief, there are several kinds of men in the world. One kind needs no training nor any particular brilliance to be a policeman. This man is against lawlessness in any form. Oddly, he may participate himself in marginal crimes, especially on a frontier where the law is vague and lax. But basically he is on the side of the law, which means the side of the people, the general run of people."

"And we're not the general run of people."

"True. Too true. At least, we have not been in the past. As to the future — would it be better for us to have a Buchanan defending us?"

"Aw, come on, Vic."

"Me a big rancher, you a respectable saloonkeeper? Money in Oswald Owens's bank?"

"And a range war on our hands?"

"To say nothing of my bride to be, the ineffable Mary." Carmer sighed. "There are, I admit, points to be considered. Yes, indeed. I think at this moment we should concentrate on acquiring cash in hand. Namely, through the engagement between Coco Bean and our Oliver."

"It's all lined up excepting the place and the referee. Plus, there's nobody knows how to set up a ring or run the fight exceptin' you and me. And we can't show."

"It would never do to know too much. We're merely amateurs backing the local pride," Carmer agreed. He peered at a mirror arranged so that it gave him a view of his barroom by way of a concealed peephole. "Let us go and speak with a man who might well relieve us of the problem."

"But who? Nobody in this town knows enough."

"Who? Why, the man who, although wearing a badge, will look the other way for this mild evasion of a stupid law. Buchanan, of course."

Strempie said, "Your Uncle Horace would be proud."

"I like to think Uncle Horace watches over us," Carmer said. "I hope they have removed the buckshot from his posterior and that he lounges in a golden chair on cushions of down, a glass of bourbon at his side."

They went into the bar, which was filling up as evening drew on. Buchanan was at the near end, sipping a beer. Oliver Green was showing his muscles to a couple of out-of-towners who had come upon the wind of rumor that a prizefight was in the making. Coco Bean was posing for Banker Owens and other backers. Stremple went to help Oliver. Carmer eased alongside Buchanan.

"Big doin's," Buchanan said affably. "Everybody loves a good fight."

"Amen," Carmer said, pouring from the house bottle of whiskey. "But we have trouble."

"That's too bad. Disappoint a whole county if anything went wrong."

"The thing is, nobody is certain of the exact London Prize Ring rules, nor how to pitch a ring," said Carmer. "With all the money being bet, the affair must be properly staged, or there'll be another riot."

"You're right about that." Buchanan appeared to engage in a slight inner struggle. Then he said reluctantly, "Happens I know about them things."

"You do?" Carmer sighed. "But you're wearing a badge."

Buchanan thought a moment more. "Tell you what. We pick a spot far away from town — up in the hills there's a little mesa — two little mesas side by side. You know?"

"Twin Flats," Carmer said. "On GG Ranch graze."

"Ah, then you can arrange with the Goodwins."

"Uh — yes, I can arrange to use the spot."

"One mesa's got some trees and brush. The other's clear — which is the one to use. Plenty of room for the sports. Might be hot, but that's the place."

Carmer said, "Then you can arrange for — uh — the ring, the rules, all that?"

"Yeah, I can do that."

Cautiously, Carmer added, "Could you referee the match?"

"You're leadin' me into trouble." But Buchanan grinned. "I could take off the badge, maybe."

"It would be acceptable to both sides. You're from out of town, you aren't betting, you're known to be a Ranger. An ideal solution."

Buchanan said, "Well, it's risky. Major Jones . . . but never mind, he's busy chasin' Indians and such. Me, I like a good prizefight as well as the next man."

"It's a deal, then. I'll speak to Owens and the other prominent citizens. You'll take over. We want this to be on the square. You're just the man for us."

"Well, I'll do my best," Buchanan said. He finished his beer. "Got to get along, now. Just let me know when everything is ready."

Carmer watched the big man, who towered over everyone in the bar, as he went sideways through the door. Had it been too easy? Was there something beneath the surface of Buchanan that was a threat? Would he call up the Rangers — but no, Jackson would report on the double if such a message went through the telegraph office. Jackson was an important cog in the machine. Jackson was pretending that his entire life savings were going down on Oliver to defeat Coco, and no one had yet paused to think that Jackson's pile could not be more than the few dollars he had not spent on women or gambled away.

It was the use of men like Jackson which set the leader apart from the rank and file,

Carmer thought. Oliver, too, and even Stremple, were puppets on his strings. And others not known to each other, obedient only to Vic Carmer, nephew of the great Uncle Horace, rest his soul in con man's heaven . . .

CHAPTER SEVEN

The early morning sun hung on a mountaintop. Buchanan sat Nightshade, a leg over the pommel, and looked from the flat top of the mesa over at its twin. They were very close together as if some glacier had come down and decapitated them in one fell slice, like a knife cutting cheese. He made a mental picture of how he would lay out the ring for the fight and that the other twin, with a few trees and some green bush, must have had a closeness to nature which this one lacked.

He rode down into town. GG cattle grazed; a cowboy lifted his hand in recognition. Buchanan responded. Days had gone by since the Hunt's arrest, and Buchanan had not heard from Major Jones, nor had he made any progress in the detection of the murderer who had done away with Gabe Goodwin. Furthermore, he had an uneasy feeling that things had been too quiet; he felt a portent of danger in Scottsville.

He stabled Nightshade. Bondi puttered around, unhearing and uncaring, a man who took part in nothing. Coco came out into the yard rubbing his eyes and started to speak but Buchanan shook his head and led the black horse into the stable.

Coco followed, saying, "That fool can't hear nothin'. I been tryin' to make him understand since we been here."

"Even the walls have ears," Buchanan told him. The stable was a litter of harness and tools. "Have you been threatened again?"

"No. They must figure I'm scared."

"Uh-huh."

"They right, big man. They plumb right."

Buchanan said, "I told you that I'll be right in there with you, wearin' my gun and all."

"That's what I'm scared of. Guns."

"Just stay that way and be ready."

"I'm ready. It's just that I'm scared."

"If you try to run away," Buchanan said, "the whole county will be after you. With a long rope."

"I'm scared of that, too." Coco reflected. "Fact is, I'm scared of everything but that big blowhead, that Oliver."

"He's just a strong boy."

"Yessir. You a strong man, too."

"I'm a Ranger," Buchanan said patiently. "I can't fight you while I'm wearin' a badge."

"Then how come you can referee?"

"There's a difference."

"I can't see it." Coco was fretful. "I druther fight you for nothin' than go through this here thing for two hundred dollars."

"You mean that's all they're giving you? Two hundred dollars? Why, there's thousands bet on the fight."

"If I live to get the two hunderd, it's all right with me," Coco said. "Too many guns. I just want us to get through here, and you and me go some place and find out who's best. No badges and no guns."

"Then behave yourself and do like I say."

"Have I got any other way to go?"

Buchanan left the dolorous fighter and went across to the Wells Fargo office. Jackson was just opening up.

"No message," said the telegrapher-clerk. "Say, you sure you know all the London prizefight rules?"

"I reckon."

"You know about the hip throw?"

"Seen it, many's the time."

"It's legal. Oliver can't lose, because he's the best at it."

"Okay."

Jackson persisted, "I seen him knock an ox stiffer than a board plank with one punch. No way to beat him, a little fella like that nigger."

"You're bettin' thataway, I hear."

"My whole life's savin's, that's how sure I am."

Buchanan asked, "Got it all up, have you?"

"You can't bet. You're the referee." Jackson was of a highly suspicious nature.

"Right," Buchanan said. He went back to the livery stable. He could spare one hundred and fifty, he thought, and still pay his local hotel bill and other expenses and have a few dollars left over. He gave the money to Coco at the rear of the barn where Bondi could not spy upon them — if indeed that worthy ever bothered to spy on anyone.

"Bet it with Jackson if you can," he told Coco. "I'll give you part of the winnin's."

"You sure I shouldn't bet on Oliver?"

"Coco, you're disappointing me," Buchanan said. "Where's your confidence?"

"In you, mister. I ain't so fond of the notion, but my confidence is in you."

"Bless you," said Buchanan. He went out onto the street again and over to Carmer's saloon. There was no one on the streets at this hour: The early risers were getting ready for the business day; the others, sleeping off last night's booze. He leaned against the front of the saloon and eyed the patched little place in the wooden wall.

He slipped out his Barlow and inserted the sharpest-pointed blade. They had used putty, and it didn't look as if anyone had gouged out the lead bullet. He smoothed over the knife mark with his thumb and went on to the hotel. The rooms were filling up with out-of-town sports, and the Basilio family were busy and happy. In the lobby he pulled up short at sight of Linda McKay.

"You didn't come calling, so I accepted another offer," she told him. "Pat sent a message."

"You just tryin' to make me jealous." He did feel a small pang that she should rush to town at Pat's suggestion.

"Maybe he wants to work out something. Between GG and us. No sense in passing up a chance. Although I don't believe he can do anything with his sister."

"Nobody can do anything with Mary," Buchanan said. "But it's right to talk peace."

"Wish me luck."

"Honey, I wish you everything in the world." He saw Pat hitching to the rail outside the hotel. "I'll duck out the back way. He don't cotton to me much lately."

"He's just a plain sorry fool," she said.

But Buchanan went out through the rear door. He circled around to the jail and entered Sheriff Master's office. It was empty. He tried the door to the cells, and it was unlocked.

Masters was looking through the bars at his one and only prisoner. Hunt was in full cry.

"I tell you, that food from Lin Chee's tastes

like washed flannel shirts. Can't I get some vittles without laundry soap stinkin' out of it?"

"Not without payin' for it," Masters said. "Lin Chee's got the town contract for jail fodder."

Buchanan said, "It's the only eatery in town, Hunt. If you had a lady friend, now, maybe she'd cook for you."

"Lady friend? Hooee! I ain't even got a man friend in this territory," Hunt said. "You hear from Major Jones? I'd as soon be in his hoosegow."

"Sure. You already broke outa there."

Hunt laughed but said no more, satisfied to wink. Masters grumbled and went back to his office.

Buchanan said, "I admire you not sayin' anything about me and Coco. You got any money?"

Hunt said, "A few holdout dollars."

"Bet it on Coco," Buchanan said.

"That ain't the way I hear it."

"Okay. Just tryin' to help. I see you got an extra mattress."

"My bones ain't fitten for jail. You know, I don't believe you got any right to hold me this long? If Jones wanted me he shoulda said so by now."

"Yeah," Buchanan said. "I got to agree. If I don't hear today, I'll think about turnin' you loose."

"That's damn decent of you," said Hunt. "Specially seein' since I'm goin' to kill you someday."

"Oh, that's okay," Buchanan said. "Everybody and his brother is out to get me one way or another. Even Major Jones."

Hunt said, "Someone'll get you. Hope it's me."

"Pat Goodwin called in Linda McKay to talk peace," Buchanan said experimentally. "Could do you out of your job at Lazy M."

"So?" Hunt seemed uninterested.

"So then what? After you kill me, that is."

Hunt said, "What have I ever done?"

"I wouldn't rightly know. I might guess, but that wouldn't be square," Buchanan said.

"You know," Hunt said, "sittin' here by my ownself, it makes a fella think some. Sure, I done some gunslingin'. But then — somebody hired me. You're really the first I ever thought to do in for personal reasons. I get to wonderin' — who's the worst, me or the ones hired me?"

"Think good about it," Buchanan advised. Then tell me the answer. For I don't know."

"Humph," Hunt said. "Leastways you ain't a know-it-all." He stretched himself on the double mattress Masters had allowed him. "You and the Nigra got somethin' goin', huh?"

"You might say. But like *you* say — they

started it. The old fight store."

"Yeah. I know about that, been in on a couple. So that's it. Carmer and Stremple?"

"Who else?"

"They been tryin' to buy me," Hunt said. "I don't work for but one man at a time. Why should they need a gun?"

"Some people are skittish when the trouble starts." But he was interested. "Anything else about them?"

"Only Mary Goodwin."

"She's goin' to marry Carmer."

"Uh-huh." Hunt wasn't surprised. "And Pat's talkin' to Linda McKay."

"Like I said."

"I wouldn't be a lawman around here right now for all the money in Texas," Hunt told him. "Come to think of it, reckon I'm better off right here in this strong old jail. Just leave me here."

"You didn't kill Gabe Goodwin," Buchanan said.

"I didn't kill Buster, neither. That Buster could sure cook up a storm. Many a hand-out he give me when I rode by. I sure wish Buster was here right now."

"You get real hungry for a skinny fella."

"Skinny ain't it, my stomach's as big as anybody's. Pappy said I eat so much it made me poor to carry it. But that laundry soap smell. Ugh!"

"I'll see you get a decent meal," Buchanan

promised. "Wouldn't want you weak or nothin' when you come gunnin' for me."

"That's white of you," Hunt said. "Who you reckon did kill Buster and Gabe?"

"You and McKay were around. What did you make of the sound of the gun that killed Gabe?" He threw the question at Hunt carelessly, quickly.

"Big gun, big noise," said Hunt without flinching. "It wasn't no new gun. Nor a six-shooter."

"Uh-huh," Buchanan said. The empty shells that had been found were a clumsy effort to disguise the real weapon, he thought. His mind had been working around that point, and now he was fairly certain of it. "Well, see you later. Rest easy. Nobody can hurt you in here."

"I hope you're right," Hunt said. "Way things are goin', you can't tell from day to day."

Buchanan went into the office, locking the big door to the cells behind him. Masters was at his desk reading the mail.

"Hunt seems okay in there."

Masters said, "He complains every hour on the hour, but he don't give trouble, if that's what you mean. He give up the idea McKay would try to bail him out."

"He's a peculiar cuss," Buchanan said. "But he ain't a backshooter nor a bushwhacker."

"Why, no. He never had that name," Masters said.

"Then who killed Buster and Gabe and took a shot at me?"

"Lordy, don't ask me. I can't learn a durn thing."

"That's what I thought." Buchanan left the sheriff at his desk.

Mary Goodwin was having another of her headaches. She sat in her father's chair, at his old desk, and stared unseeing at the tally book. She was wearing Levis, boots and a man's shirt. She put a hand to her head and sighed, leaning back. Dr. Gill had not been able to do anything for her; his pills had not worked. She reached into a drawer, took out her father's whiskey bottle and drank from the neck, quickly, guiltily wiping her mouth. At first it had stung and choked her, but now it slid down her throat and made her feel better for the moment.

There was the sound of horses. She looked out the window and saw four men, strangers, riding in. She gripped the butt of her father's six-gun, but Dungan came from the corral, swaggering like a banty rooster. The men hallooed him and dismounted.

They were all big men, making Dungan seem a tiny, menacing doll with his holstered big Colt's revolvers. He shook hands with them and motioned toward the house. Mary got up and went out on the porch.

Dungan said excitedly, "Here they are, Miss Mary. Four of the very best. Cactus, Akili Ike, Jorey and Montana. This here is Miss Mary, my boss."

They scraped and bowed and took off their hats. It was impossible to tell them apart. They were all gunnies: all muscular, tough brutes. She wondered what they were doing on GG Ranch. Galloway, Gomez and Perry were enough hands until roundup time.

Dungan said, "A hundred apiece, remember? Like you said? No wages, just a hundred apiece. They stay 'til the job is done."

She dared not ask what job he meant. She forgot too many details lately. She did remember agreeing that they needed fighters to avenge her father . . .

That was it. To clean out Lazy M and kill her father's murderer. The flame lit up in her brain.

"Yes. Right. I have the money."

She went inside to her father's safe and removed four hundred dollars. She carried the money out and gave it to Dungan. Then she remembered something else — Pat, her brother, was in town to meet with Linda McKay.

She said briskly, "We'll ride into town."

"Now?" Dungan was surprised but pleased. "Right now?"

"The McKay gal," Mary said. "That damn pulin' brother of mine. We'll give 'em a lesson."

"You goin' to shoot *them?*"

"No. Just show them."

"Yes, Miss Mary," Dungan said. "I'll saddle up for you."

He beckoned to the quartet, and they walked toward the corral while he explained the situation. He was happy as a bug in a rug with his assignment, bossing four tough ones with the beautiful Miss Mary giving the orders from the top. He had never been quite so happy.

Mary went back into the house for her sombrero. She hesitated, then dashed into the office and took another swig of the whiskey. Now things seemed clear: She was going to straighten out her weakling brother and Linda McKay . . . straighten them out . . .

In the lobby of the hotel, Linda McKay and Pat Goodwin sat in a far corner and spoke in low voices, glaring at one another. She was angry, he was sullen and defiant.

"Why did you call me in here?" she demanded.

"To put some sense in your head."

"By accusing me of — of everything?"

"By telling you Buchanan is just a big

saddle bum, a good fella, but nobody for you."

She said, "Pat Goodwin, when you are half the man Buchanan is — write me a letter and tell me about it."

"Now what does that mean?"

"It means you let that sister of yours lead you around by the nose. That you half believe my father killed your father."

He said, reluctantly, "No. I don't believe that."

"Nor did any other Lazy M man!"

"Hunt's no backshooter," he muttered. "Reckon you're right about that."

"Ask Buchanan, if you don't believe me."

"Buchanan! That faker's no lawman. He's a big, tough drifter, that's what he is. I know Buchanan."

"Not half as well as he knows you! He's sorry for you. He can see what you're up against. Mary and that Vic Carmer."

"You should talk about Carmer!"

"All right. When he first came to town I thought he was good company."

"Buggy ridin' with him. Barn dancin' with him."

"I swear, Pat Goodwin, you are a namby-pamby cry-baby. You wouldn't ask me yourself because your father and sister made such a fuss. Then you complain because I went out and had such a good time!"

"I was argufyin' with them about you. I

left home on account of you."

"A lot of good that did me, you leaving home. I don't understand it. Everybody around here says you were a fine young fellow, had a lot of gumption and guts. Stood up to your father. But that was when Mary was away, wasn't it? When she was back East. I swear, I believe you're scared of your own sister."

He began a hot reply, then a haunted expression settled on his features. "Linda — maybe I am. She — she's sick. I don't know. She's hexed or somethin'. She says Pa won't rest in his grave until she finds his murderer. It ain't — it ain't right, the way she is."

She relented. "I didn't mean you were actually scared. I don't believe you're a coward, Pat. I know better. But that Dungan — he's far worse than Hunt."

"She and Dungan — that's another thing. They whisper together. He follows her, every step she takes. It's plain unhealthy."

"Why don't you do something about it?"

"She's my sister. Half owner of GG Ranch, half owner of everything. I don't know what to do," he confessed from the depths of his misery. "I want peace between us and Lazy M. It's the only way this country'll ever make it. I want . . ."

There were a rattle of spurs and a clank of guns as Dungan walked into the hotel, smirking at them and removing his hat. "Miss McKay . . . Mr. Pat . . . you're wanted outside."

"Who wants us?" Pat demanded.

"Just your own sister," Dungan whined. "She's got some friends she wants you to meet. Both of you, like, she told me."

Linda said, "I don't care to meet any of her friends."

"We'd better humor her," Pat whispered. "Maybe she's come to her senses. Maybe she realizes she's wrong."

"That, I cannot believe," Linda said. Still, she did want peace between the ranches, between the families. She was feeling tender toward Pat since his confession of a few moments before. She saw his problem, sensed his suffering. She was a bit ashamed of having ridden out with Vic Carmer in order to make Pat jealous. She got up and followed the two men onto the veranda of the hotel.

The sun was bright after the dimness of the lobby, and at first her vision was impaired. Then she heard a dull thud and saw Pat stagger and fall down the steps onto the boardwalk. She turned to run back inside, but Dungan and a big man behind her twisted her arm and forced her down alongside the fallen Pat.

Then she saw Mary Goodwin in her boots and Levis, a riding crop in her hand. Mary was staring out of her great wild eyes, feet spread apart, her teeth showing between parted red lips. There were other men with drawn guns flanking Mary and covering the town. Dungan was chuckling like an evil little barnyard fowl.

The gunbearers were strangers to Linda, and on sight she knew that she would not care to know them. The street was almost deserted. Those in view were held motionless under the weapons of Dungan and the others. Vic Carmer strolled out of his saloon and stood as though transfixed, staring at his affianced lady. Pat lay immobile under the feet of the big man who had clubbed him down, a small trickle of blood running down one cheek.

The sight of Pat's blood, his white face still and vacant; the glee of the midget Dungan and the brutal visages of the henchmen brought her to her feet and down the steps of the veranda toward Mary Goodwin. She felt no fear, only a cold rage.

They faced each other, the tall, full-bodied young woman in her man's attire and the tiny girl in her divided skirt, soft boots, bolero jacket and silken blouse. Carmer took two steps and cried out.

"No, Mary! No!"

"Stay out of this, darling." Mary's deep voice was curiously similar to that of her late father. "This is between me and that one. Her men killed my Pa. I aim to show her a thing or two."

She slapped the whip into her left palm. Her eyes were wide, her chin thrust out.

Linda said, "You're a fool, Mary."

Carmer took one more step and one of the gunmen raised a revolver. Carmer stopped, looking for help and finding none. Stremple looked out of the barroom but remained indoors.

Mary Goodwin said, "I'm goin' to give you a whuppin', Linda McKay. I'm goin' to make you a disgrace in the country. I'm goin' to make your name a household word. People will laugh, Linda McKay. They'll say you got your comeuppance."

Before anyone could grab her and hold her for the whip, Linda McKay charged. She was small — she weighed no more than one hundred pounds as she stood — but she put down her head and plunged toward Mary Goodwin.

The bigger woman, surprised, tried to back away. Her heel caught, and she stumbled. Linda hit her amidships and knocked her into the dust of the street. The whip flew out of Mary's grasp. Linda seized the red hair of the raging girl and began beating Mary's head against the ground.

Dungan cackled, dancing around, but the action was so fast and so close that he dared not interfere, because of the danger of harming his lady boss. The gunmen, caught off-balance by a situation with which they had no experience, continued to menace the citizenry, and now the street was filling up with local people and the out-of-town sports. Fred Masters came running and was stopped at gunpoint.

Mary scratched at Linda's face but missed when the little girl buried her head between her adversary's ample bosoms. Using superior weight, Mary kicked and rolled over. With instinctive reaction, Linda doubled up and elbowed her way free, smashing one tiny fist into Mary's left eye.

They came to their feet, and Mary reached to seize her smaller opponent. Linda ducked and sidestepped, then charged again. Her head struck Mary in the midriff, and again they went down. Now a dust cloud enveloped them. When it cleared, Linda could be seen on the top, whaling away with both hands. Mary had her arms closed about her face and was bucking like a bronco. Dungan started for them, unable to bear the sight of his adored boss being soundly whipped by the little McKay girl.

Buchanan came on the run from Bondi's, where he had been conferring with Coco Bean. The prizefighter came behind him. One of the gunmen swung around. Buchanan knocked the weapon from his hand and ran on.

The strange gunny bent to pick up his weapon. Coco kicked him in the head and proceeded, cautiously, behind Buchanan. Carmer suddenly produced his derringer, and as a second imported badman aimed at Buchanan, he shot the man in the belly. There was a loud and agonized groan, and then Dungan came around with both guns drawn.

Buchanan's long legs had carried him close enough for action. Once more, he plucked Dungan from terra firma and shook him. The guns rattled like clothespins in a wind. Coco hit a third gunman with his right hand, and the man lost all interest in the proceedings. Carmer shouted for everyone to hold still.

Masters dove into the sheriff's office under cover of the excitement and came out with a greener in his hands. Stremple appeared with a six-shooter. People lost their fear. The fourth gunman lost interest and holstered his revolver. Buchanan tossed Dungan away as though he were a useless hunk of material, and the little fellow landed alongside Coco, who dropped a fist on his head with such force that the midget appeared to be driven into the earth.

Buchanan now applied himself to the core of the disturbance. He leaned gingerly into the billowing dust cloud, seeking a handhold to break loose the two ladies.

At this moment, Mary's superior weight and strength began to prevail. She kicked high in turning over the smaller girl. One boot heel caught Buchanan in the jaw and drove him to the boardwalk, where he sat down with great loss of dignity. Pat Goodwin opened an eye and mumbled, "What the hell's goin' on here?"

"A cat fight. Which is considerable worse'n a dog fight," Buchanan told him.

Mary was now seeking a grip on Linda's throat. She succeeded in tearing the bolero jacket and ripping loose the silken shirt. Women gasped and men stared. Buchanan rose and went back to the fray.

A clawing set of fingernails raked his jawline. Linda was ripping at Mary Goodwin's eyes. Buchanan got hold of Mary, found that he had her by the back of her pants and sought to change the hold, in the interest of propriety. He was soundly kicked below the belt by Linda. The breath went out of him for a moment.

Then he became angry. He reached with both hands. Where he grabbed he did not know or care. He yanked hard, and the two women came apart. He jerked them again. They came to their feet, hair streaming, faces caked with dirt, clothing ripped to shreds. He held them at arm's length until the dust died down.

Then he said, "You oughta see yourselves.

Gals, you are sure a mess."

It was like throwing cold water on a dog fight. Mary had lost all the buttons on her man's shirt. Linda was even more exposed through the bodice of her undergarment. In Buchanan's grasp, they both began to wriggle and weep. He led them toward the hotel, right up to the door, their feet barely touching the ground as they went. He shoved them toward the staring Basilio family.

"Keep 'em apart and bathe 'em," he said. "There'll be clothes for 'em by the time they're cleaned up and settled down . . . Mary, if you start up again I'm goin' to turn you over and spank you right before God and everybody."

They did not seem to hear him. They scooted out of sight, and Buchanan turned to survey the field of battle. Dungan was just coming to consciousness. Buchanan put a finger on him and spun him at Masters.

"Better jail this one. What about the others?"

Masters said, "Doc Gill just told us one of 'em's dead."

Buchanan walked to where lay the body of the gunman slain by Carmer. "Why, it's Akili Ike Sable. Now what was he doin' hereabouts?"

"Came in with Dungan and them," said

Masters. Loyal in his fashion, he was unwilling to name a Goodwin.

Buchanan looked around. "Cactus, Jorey, Montana. Dungan, you really pick the dandies, now, don't you?"

"I'm gonna kill you before the week is out," Dungan swore. "I'm gonna peg your hide on the barn door."

"Yeah," Buchanan said. "But not this week. You wouldn't want to spoil the prizefight, now would you?"

Masters said, "Come on, Dungan. You can have fun with your old pal Hunt."

Pat Goodwin, shaky and pale, came to them. "Mary'll bail him out in the morning, you know that. What happened, anyway?"

"Your sister had you knocked out," Masters said. "Hate to say it, Pat, but you better watch out for her." He marched off to the jail, prodding Dungan before him.

Coco, Buchanan noted, had wisely vanished after doing his part. Carmer stood against the wall of his saloon, silent, his face smooth and blank.

Buchanan said, "Reckon I owe you one. Akili never did cotton much to me. He'd have liked gettin' a free shot."

Carmer said, "Any time, Buchanan."

"Can't you do anything about Mary?" Buchanan asked.

"I tried."

Buchanan shook his head. "All I got to

say is — you marry her, and you'll earn every head of beef on GG Ranch."

Carmer did not alter expression. "A time and a place for everything, isn't there?"

"If the time ever comes."

"Drinks are on me."

Buchanan said, "Not right now. There's a couple things I got to do. But the fight'll come off on time. I got the posts and the rope. Need somebody to dig postholes. You might see to that."

"I wouldn't know how." Carmer lied with a straight face.

"Just get the labor, I'll oversee the job." Buchanan could dissemble as well as the saloonkeeper.

Men came and removed the body of Akili Ike. He would find his resting place on Boot Hill before nightfall, with no mourners. It was an end he had sought, Buchanan thought as he went toward the hotel with Pat at his elbow. They all went looking for trouble, and when it came they took it this way or that according to their natures. Most of them died game with their boots on. Some wept at the hanging tree, some went weak-kneed at the final curtain, but the gunnies all came to it sooner or later. They were a breed apart: They did not care about the victims, they cared little about a cause; they caught the fever and they were killers; and that was the way they lived.

And died, he added.

He said to Pat, "You know, it looked to me, there, like Linda was givin' as good or better than she was receivin'."

Pat felt the lump on his head. "And there I was, out like a lamp."

"Just as well," Buchanan consoled him. "Now neither of 'em can accuse you. Let 'em howl at me."

"For what?" Pat was astounded. "You saved them both from doin' anything worse than they already did."

"What could be worse? They got themselves all untidy in public," Buchanan said out of his wisdom. "They got to blame somebody, and it's got to be a man."

CHAPTER EIGHT

Because the hotel was crowded with the out-of-town people come to the prize-fight, they used Buchanan's room. Linda was now attired in a boy's shirt, and her damp hair was caught back beneath a *rebozoa.* There wasn't a mark on her face, although she complained about bruises on various parts of her small body.

Pat said miserably, "I feel like a plain fool."

"They hurt you," she said softly.

He touched the patch applied by Doc Gill. "Maybe they knocked some sense into my thick head."

"I hope so," Buchanan said. "Mary took off before I could get to her. She bamboozled Masters into givin' bail to Dungan and took the other three and went to the ranch. I didn't want to turn those customers all over to Fred. He ain't up to a gang like that."

"No. He means good, but he can't handle it," Pat said. "Mary'll make more trouble. Reckon I ought to go home and keep an eye on 'em."

"No," Linda said, "they could kill you. Dungan would do it in a minute."

"Mary wouldn't go that far." But Pat said it without conviction.

"Mary's wrong in the head," Linda told him. "She wanted to kill me, I can tell you that."

"She truly believes Lazy M killed Pa," Pat said.

"She's got some others believin' it," Buchanan told them. "Coco knows. People talk around him — they don't think a black prizefighter's a human, somehow or other. He hears all kinds of stuff. Mary hollers so loud and long, and Dungan with her, she's got some folks swallowin' the notion. I been trying to cool things off here and there. It ain't easy."

"She can make fierce trouble if she gets people believin' her way," Pat said. "Only thing to do is find out who did kill Buster and Pa."

"And took that shot at you or me."

"You think it could've been at me?" Pat was surprised. Then he said, "Hey, that puts a different face on it, huh?"

"It's got too many faces now," Buchanan said. "I'm goin' to leave you two here for a while. Don't go home, either of you, until I talk to you, understand?"

Linda said, "I've already sent a boy out to tell father I won't be home." She hesitated, flushed. "I thought — I thought Pat might need me."

"Uh-huh," Buchanan said. "Well, it was nice flirtin' with you, darlin'."

He ducked out the door before either of them could answer. He walked on the street, where there were people talking in little tight knots, local people discussing the fight between the girls. They looked at him with eyes of hometowners regarding an outsider. He went down to the livery stable and climbed to the loft where Coco slept. At the top of the ladder he paused, looking toward the cleared space among the neatly stacked bales of hay and straw to where Coco sat on the edge of the cot, head in hands, staring out through the single window.

There was an old utility cabinet which Coco had found in the rubbish of the stable below and which he had refinished, rubbing it so that the beautiful grain came through the paint. In it hung the rolled-neck sweaters and heavy tight pants for training, Coco's work garments; two shirts Buchanan had brought for him; a pair of Levis not yet worn in and an extra pair of boots, of which Coco was inordinately proud. Everything was in apple-pie order.

Buchanan was held still by a sudden new thought: This was a man. Just now he had acted despite his horror and fear of gunplay. He had been superb — and he had vanished without waiting to hear praise he suspected would not be forthcoming from the local citizens. This was a man, simple and direct but worthy. He would allow the people to feel his muscles, debate about his chances in the ring and talk around him and over him but seldom at him. And Coco knew — and now it struck Buchanan full, hard force — that he was a black man and, therefore, one apart.

In Buchanan's heart there was a cry for justice, even as he knew there was no justice. He climbed into the loft. Coco turned to stare a moment, then his gaze went back to the scene beyond the window.

"You did real great," Buchanan said in a tone he had not used before, he realized. "You were fine out there."

"That Carmer." Coco spoke deep in his throat.

"Well, the man, Akili, he was goin' to backshoot me."

"Nossuh," Coco said. "I had him lined up."

"Carmer didn't know that, maybe."

"He don't care. Not nohow. He ups with that teensy gun, and he shoots the man. Guns!"

"It's a hard country, and guns are needed," Buchanan said. "I'm against them, too. But it'll take time, lots more people, more laws, to do away with the guns."

"Till then, people get shot."

"I'm afraid so."

"Nossuh, I ain't never goin' to like it. I scared."

"You're not scared. You're nervous about guns, but you proved today you're not scared."

Coco said, "You and me right up there in that ring. Spooky voice says I am to lay down. I don't. You and me, we nothin' but targets. Just shootin' targets."

"I aim to take care of that."

"Nobody took care of them that was shot before. Nobody took care of him what shot at you. Shootin', that's the way of things."

"They won't shoot you, I promise." But he did not really know they would not. He was nearing a conclusion, one that he could not state even to himself, and he certainly was not sure they would not be cut down when Coco refused to obey orders.

"Mebbe I can't whup this big man. He strong. He knock down horses, bulls, they say."

"Maybe you can't."

"I look at that man there, that deafy one." Coco pointed. Buchanan went to the window and looked out at Bondi, who was forking manure into a pit. "He don't have no truck with nothin'. He don't even know there was a shootin'. Maybe the Lawd was good to him. He don't have to know."

Buchanan made a trumpet of his hands and yelled in a voice like thunder, "Hey, Bondi, look out!"

The man did not look up, the fork continued to toss the manure. Buchanan hunkered down alongside Coco and said, "Supposin' a man with a knife or a gun had been creepin' up on Bondi just now. He don't hear me. He's dead."

"He still don't know," Coco said simply. "He never know what hit him."

Buchanan said, "Okay. If that's the way you think, I got no argument. Forget it. Now, what about this Oliver Green? They says he rassles a bit."

"I hear that. I don't like it nohow."

"A fighter's no good off his feet."

"You knows that."

"You have to be ready for the hip throw and all."

"I am as ready as I can get," Coco said. "Remember, mister, I'm a black man. Nobody ever give me the best of it. I got to be ready."

"Yeah," Buchanan said. Again he felt sympathy for the prizefighter. "Look, you need anything? Lin Chee feedin' you good?"

Coco's eyes glowed. "Lin Chee feeds me in his own kitchen. I sit down at the table with his own wife. Lin Chee's the best part of this whole thing we got here."

"Okay. You get a chance to bet our money?"

"I was comin' from there when the fuss

started. That Jackson, he ain't no real kind of a man."

"True." Buchanan patted the fighter's shoulder. "I do thank you for what you did."

Coco did not look up. He mumbled, "Aw — you welcome."

Buchanan went down the ladder. Coco sat a long while, staring at Bondi. After the manure was piled, the man went to the house in the rear — a filthy cabin — and closed the door. Coco smiled then, thinking how much better off he was than the livery man.

Then he frowned, wondering why he felt that way, and why he suddenly didn't have any great desire to beat up on Buchanan.

In the sheriff's office, Masters refused to meet Buchanan's eyes. "When Mary comes atcha like that — there wasn't any way to get out of takin' bail. The judge won't be around the circuit for a month. It was no use tryin' to hold Dungan."

"He hired the other gunnies," Buchanan said. "There'll be more trouble, Fred."

"Mary can make enough trouble any time."

"It's your town to law," Buchanan said. "What about Carmer?"

"The jury met and cleared him in five minutes. Doc Gill's the coroner, no use wastin' time on that."

"Uh-huh," Buchanan said. "Let me talk to Hunt."

"Key's on the hook." Masters was despondent. "You think I did wrong."

"I'd like to have Dungan in jail for a while."

"This is my last term," Masters said. "Job's gettin' to be too much, the GG bunch and the Lazy M bunch and the killin's and all. I don't care to mess with such doin's. Only ran because nobody else wanted the job, and Gabe asked me to."

"Don't blame you," Buchanan said. "This lawin' is another thing. Don't know what I'm doin' in the midst of it, neither. But here I am — and here I stay 'til it's over."

"There'll be killin' and more killin'."

"That's what my friend Coco says."

"Your friend . . . oh, you mean the nigger."

"He's got to be a friend. Man all alone in a strange town, he needs a friend."

"Reckon so." Masters was not interested.

Buchanan unlocked the big door and went into the cells. Hunt was stretched out, his hat tilted over the blade of his sharp nose.

"Did Fred tell you about it?" Buchanan asked.

"Uh-huh. Akili Ike and who else?"

"Cactus, Jorey and Montana."

"You didn't get none of them?"

"Had some troubles with the gals. And how did you get along with Dungan?"

"It was right cute. He thinks we killed Gabe, all right. Tried to get between the bars and grab me."

"He and Mary are somewhat *loco*. Mind spendin' one more night in here?"

"I mind like hell. But what can I do?"

"Got to make last-minute arrangements about the prizefight," Buchanan said.

"Uh-huh. Say, the Basilios sent me one good meal. Real soup, no soap. Thanks."

"Thank them."

"You paid for it. That cunnin' little Maria told me."

"You keep your hands off that kid."

"Why, Buchanan, shame on you for thinkin' on such a thing," Hunt said.

Buchanan grinned at him. "Had to give myself a strong talkin' to about her. I don't figure you're any better than me."

Hunt said, "You'll learn. Wait'll I get my chance."

"Oh, sure," Buchanan said. "I ain't forgettin'."

"How about that fight?"

"What do you mean?"

"Well, how you goin' to handle things?"

"I might just tell you that. Tomorrow."

"Don't you go getting me into it. I got my own problems. I ain't one for prizefights, there's no guns in it."

"Coco, he's just the other way around. You and Coco, you wouldn't agree at all."

Hunt chuckled. "I dunno. He's a nice, likable Nigra, at that. Somethin' about him — like a nice kid."

"He's brighter than you think. And he's dead game."

"You tryin' to tell me somethin', Buchanan?"

"I been tryin' to tell you things. All you think about is that fast gun of yours."

"I'll show you that fast gun someday," said Hunt comfortably. "It'll be the last thing you see."

"You keep saying that. If you had any brains under your hat, you'd have other things on your mind. Like Dungan, Cactus, Jorey and Montana."

"You let me out of here, and I'll take care of them."

"One at a time or all at once?"

"It don't matter nohow. You stop to think if they raid Lazy M you're responsible for what happens to those innocent souls out there?"

"Just what I have been ponderin'," Buchanan said. "But with the prizefight and all the strangers in town it ain't likely. Not yet."

"I figured that much."

"And I'm goin' to let you out for the fight. Major Jones don't seem interested noway in either of us. So you can protect the innocent."

"Uh-huh."

"You take McKay's wages."

"Right. That's why it's 'uh-huh.' Obie Deal, I can make a fighter outa him and Madigan and Bender and all. I got a talent for makin' people fight. Which you will see when it comes down to you and me."

"I look forward to the day," Buchanan said. "Y' see, I'm so worried and so scared, it'll be a relief to get it over."

"Bull feathers," Hunt said.

"You just rest easy 'til tomorrow."

"I got nothin' much planned." He tilted the hat down over his eyes. "Never knew a man could sleep so much."

Buchanan started to leave, paused. "Hunt?"

"Yeah?"

"If you nor McKay didn't kill Gabe and I didn't — then who did?"

"You're the lawman."

"You got an idea who might've done it?"

"I ain't a damn fool altogether."

"What about it?"

Hunt said, "I'm in jail."

"What about it when you get out?"

"You can't arrest a man without proof, can you?"

"Course not."

"Me, I got my ways. I can't shoot a man without the proof."

Buchanan said, "See you tomorrow, Hunt."

"I'll be here."

Buchanan left the jail, walked down the street and went into Vic Carmer's saloon. There were more people from out of town. Stremple and Green were busy as one-armed paperhangers serving drinks. Carmer was at his usual place at the end of the long bar.

Buchanan said, "Drink's on me."

"That's okay," Carmer said. "Think nothing of it."

"You know the man you shot?"

"No. He was fixing to backshoot you is all I know."

"Bad fella," Buchanan said. "Your lady friend brought in some real bad ones."

"She failed to consult me."

"That's kind of funny, ain't it?"

"In a way." Carmer hesitated. "After all, she does believe that Lazy M is responsible for Gabe's death. She believes that either GG or Lazy M has to perish."

"And you?"

Reluctantly, Carmer said, "Lazy M has the motive. Both McKay and Hunt were around the night it happened."

"And Buster was killed by an Indian?"

"I don't know," Carmer said. "I wouldn't accuse anyone. It's really not my business, you know."

"But you're going to marry Mary Goodwin."

"That has nothing to do with the matter,

now, has it?" Carmer asked. "You're not quizzing me, are you?"

"Just lookin' for information," Buchanan said. "It's a mighty scarce article around here."

"Masters is little help," Carmer said. "Any chance the Rangers will take a hand?"

"Haven't heard," Buchanan said.

"Seems like they would attempt to prevent trouble before it happens."

"Major Jones is right busy," said Buchanan. He lifted his beer. "Well, here's thankin' you again. Might've saved my life."

"That was my intention," Carmer said, bowing slightly. "We have need for a man like you. By the way, is everything ready for the fight day after tomorrow?"

"The postholes will be dug this afternoon," Buchanan said. "Coco tells me he's ready."

"Then we'll look forward to it. Biggest event ever took place here in Scottsville."

"Far as that's concerned, it's a good thing Major Jones didn't take it into his head to come this way."

"Right. It'll be over and history before he can stop it," Carmer said. "After all, it's harmless fun."

"Harmless if you ain't in there buttin' heads," Buchanan said. "See you tomorrow."

Men from out of town, local people — everyone — made a path for Buchanan as he eased his way to the door. They stared up at him, wondering at his scarred face, his enormous spread of shoulder, his huge hands. Even Oliver Green lost his truculence, as Buchanan stopped to ask him how he felt, and was able to mumble only a weak reply. In addition to his physical presence, Buchanan had taken on the aura of the man of the hour, the referee officially in charge of the biggest sporting event of that or any other year.

He went over to the livery stable. Bondi was puttering around in the mysterious and confusing clutter of the littered barn. There were dozens of pegs on the wall. There were boxes and crates, and the corners had been stacked with an amazing conglomeration of articles which to the casual eye seemed of no use whatever. Buchanan did not bother to try to communicate with the deaf man. He saddled Nightshade and led him out into the yard. Coco was not in sight. Probably running in the hills, Buchanan thought, keeping his legs in shape.

He rode out toward Lazy M. He wanted McKay and his people to know about the men brought in by Mary Goodwin. It was like a warning about a plague of locusts or an invasion by savage Indians. It was only fair that McKay be forewarned.

Carmer and Stremple sat for a moment

in the office of the saloon. Stremple was wiping his forehead and taking a breather from the arduous tending of the bar.

"That was a close one today," he said. "You thought mighty fast."

"That's my forte," Carmer said. "I think fast."

"None of the rest of 'em know us."

"No. Only Akili. I saw it in his eyes when I shot him."

"You should have put one in his head. He might have talked."

"No. The .45 caliber pure lead bullet in the gut will give any man enough to think upon as he dies."

"I sure give you credit. Too bad, though. He would've got rid of Buchanan."

"No. The Nigra was right there. But Coco would only have stunned him. He had to die."

Stremple asked curiously, "I never knew you to kill before. How many have you downed?"

"He was the first," Carmer said.

"I believe you. It didn't faze you any?"

"None at all." Carmer sounded faintly surprised. "It was like exterminating a rattlesnake. Akili was no good to anyone and he was ruination to us."

"I might have got him with the rifle, but I just didn't think quick enough. It's a pleasure to work with you, Vic."

"How much have we bet on the fight?"

"Every spare dime we own."

"Yes. I thought so. You see? Akili had to go."

Stremple grinned. "And after all, we couldn't have our referee killed, could we?"

"Buchanan is not a stupid man. But he is simple. Now that I cut down a man trying to backshoot him, Buchanan believes in me."

"I figured that. After it was over." Stremple shook his head. "You are a pure marvel, Vic."

"Thank you."

"You think everything will be okay to-night?"

"There will be more drunks than Scottsville ever saw. They'll be whooping it up in their own fashion."

"Yeah, that's right."

"Tonight for the first time since we opened here I shall be behind the bar, helping you and Oliver."

"We can use the help."

"Yes."

"You really have a head on you. Sometimes I have had my doubts. This thing is pretty risky. And you marryin' that crazy lady. But you sure know what you're doing."

"Up until that point." Carmer winced. "That is for the future to decide."

"You having doubts about that, too?"

"Women is a creature not predictable," Carmer said. "We have always bet on sure things."

"But what about you owning the ranch and all that?"

"I want it," Carmer said frankly. "I want always to bet on the sure thing. It is a golden opportunity. Politics — why, we were born for politics. We could go far, Stremple. There is no limit to where we could rise. That is, if we were established."

"Some people might remember some things."

"Once you have arrived people forget. Or they don't care. Or they think it was youthful folly, not to be held against a rich successful man. That part is of no interest to me. It is getting to the goal, acquiring both GG and Lazy M, solidifying a position. Electing you mayor of Scottsville."

"Why, they don't even have a mayor."

"They will, Stremple, they will."

"You sure do have big ideas in that head of yours."

"I'm glad you recognize the fact. I wouldn't want you harboring those little doubts, Stremple."

"Don't worry about me."

"I don't."

"I mean, I'm on your side, all the way."

"There isn't any other way for you," Carmer said gently. "Never forget that. Not even for a moment."

"Not me. I know when I'm well off."

"Yes. You always have."

"Well, just you remember." Stremple seemed hurt. "Since we joined up, with half the money put up by me, I never tried to interfere with your schemes. Did I?"

"No, you didn't. Isn't that wonderful?"

"Well, here we are. And you've got the big plans. I think it's good."

"Continue to hold the faith." Carmer dismissed him with a smile and a wave of the hand. Stremple went slowly, pausing with chin on shoulder then closing the door softly behind him.

Stremple was invaluable, but it would never do to let the man know it, Carmer thought. Uncle Horace had taught him how to handle men of lesser intelligence . . . and more physical initiative and courage. It did not pay to be brave. Bravery was stupidity, Uncle Horace always said. It did pay to hire the brave. Great nations hired brave men to fight their wars.

Stremple was smart enough. He had been successful in his minor field of fleecing the yokels, and he had been ambitious and realistic enough to realize that Carmer possessed the superior background and intelligence. The partnership had been profitable to both.

But now it was time to cogitate. Uncle Horace's weakness had been women. Face it, he had met his death at the hands of a woman. The widow could not have been any more inclined to violence than Mary Goodwin.

Pat Goodwin was not a factor with which he would have to contend, he believed. The young man had no real incentive: he was mooning after the McKay fluff, he was his mother's son, he had not the iron of his father. It was the woman who presented the problem.

Could he manage her? Was she as susceptible to the tender aspects of the love she professed? Could she be dominated by her love for Vic Carmer?

Another man might, egotistically, believe so. Carmer had seen Uncle Horace in action, and at times he had prevailed. But these had been take-the-cash-and-run situations. What Carmer wanted was permanence, a position. He had not been wildly dreaming when he spoke to Stremple of politics. A study of frontier government and its representatives had convinced him that he had a niche to fill. The men in the seat of government in Austin had not impressed him.

It would be, he thought, highly humorous if he could win a position from which he could direct the Texas Rangers to his own ends.

Still, he was a cautious man. He could scheme; he could bind men to him and make them do his bidding. But he was skeptical of women. They could not be trusted. They twisted and turned and moved unexpectedly, without reason. It would take a lot of thinking to come to a decision as to what to do about Mary Goodwin. If she continued to ride around in men's clothing with cutthroats in attendance, she might well be killed by a stray bullet, and this would mean the end of Carmer's overall plan. It was necessary to act quickly. After the prizefight he would have all the cash he needed in his hands, he decided. He could postpone it until after the fight.

Meantime, there were things to be accomplished.

At night they were still coming in. The news of the prizefight had spread to the farthest nooks of the county, and people starved for entertainment made haste to be on hand early so that they might not miss anything that went on. They came on horseback and in all sorts of vehicles, from farm wagons carrying whole families to carriages drawn by handsome matched teams.

The hotel was long since filled, men sleeping triple and even quadruple in the rooms. The Basilios had set up a restaurant under canvas in the back yard because Lin Chee couldn't possibly serve everyone, even with help from cousins imported in great haste from El Paso. Now the farmers and cowboys were setting up housekeeping on the plains surrounding the town. Every night, the small town was riotous with the sound of good-natured merrymaking. It was a holiday mood, and even Fred Masters was not put to task to keep the peace.

Buchanan, who had been up at dawn and who had vigorously defended the right of a Ranger to a private room, was asleep against the busy morrow.

Hunt lay on his cot in the jail and told himself he was glad to be out of the noise and confusion. He was not a man for crowds; he felt uneasy in a mob. He did not drink a lot. He did not gamble. That is, not unless he knew with whom he was tilting and felt that he had an edge.

He was half asleep when the shot sounded. There had been very little shooting, and he wondered who had started it so close to the jail. He hoped it wasn't the Lazy M and GG Ranch starting a ruckus when he was not present to cut down on Dungan. He had been planning how he would take that little monster, firing right down through the top of his ridiculous wide-brimmed, too big hat.

He was still on the cot when the big door

to the office opened. Therefore, he did not glimpse the figure which bent its knees, aimed with care and slid a key the length of the cell block so that it came within his reach.

He did hear the voice which whispered loudly, "You better take off before they find him, Hunt. Otherwise they'll hang you right quick."

He came off the cot. There was no one in sight. He leaned down and picked up the key. Working from behind the bars, he managed to unlock the cell. He slipped into the corridor, ran to the big door and peered through the doorway into the office.

Fred Masters lay on his belly. He had been shot in the back. There was a Colt's revolver on the desk.

Hunt moved fast. He picked up the gun. It was his; there was his mark on the butt. His belt hung on a peg. There was an empty shell in the chambers of his Colt's.

Hunt blew out the single lamp in the office. He made certain that the sheriff was dead. He sat on his heels inside the door that led to the street and thought it through.

The killer wanted him out of town. There could be several reasons.

Or the killer wanted him back with Lazy M, either to stir up trouble, to seek protection or to harm the Goodwin crowd.

Or the killer simply wanted Masters dead, local law strangled and Hunt a fugitive suspected of the murder.

Or the killer was waiting to get him outdoors, shoot him and proclaim him the murderer, thus killing two birds with one stone.

It occurred to him that right now he would welcome the presence of only one man — Buchanan. This was laughable, but it happened to be true. He had to move or be lynched; the whisperer had been one hundred percent right about that. If Buchanan knew the facts, it would be wise to be guided by the big man's advice.

He looked around the office. There was no rear exit to the building — prevention against prisoners leaving by the back door. In the dimness, Hunt strapped on his holster and reloaded the six-gun. He touched the brim of his hat, tipping it in characteristic fashion down over his sharp nose. He went to the door, took a deep breath, opened it and walked boldly into the throng of people milling up and down the main street of Scottsville.

CHAPTER NINE

Buchanan sat in the bottoms of his long summer underwear and stared at his bare feet. Hunt sat on the chair with his hat now pushed back on his head.

"Yeah," Buchanan said. "I can see what you got in mind."

"It ain't the Goodwin crowd, I don't think. Exceptin' Dungan, and I don't think he's got pea brains. There's no one of 'em would pull a stunt like this."

"You got an idea. I got an idea. Want to bet we can't prove a thing?"

"No bet. This here is both smart and somewhat *loco*. This whole thing is wild and woolly."

"Masters," Buchanan said. "Wasn't for this rangdoodle, he coulda lived all his life without trouble. He was a man didn't go lookin' for bears in the brush."

"He wasn't a bad *hombre* at all," Hunt conceded. "Treated me right good, let me have a second mattress and all. I figured you'd know I didn't backshoot a man like Masters."

"That's about all I do know," Buchanan

confessed. "I got to get you to cover. I got to take over for Masters. You stop to think I'm now the only law in Scottsville?"

"Good thing you got a little sleep." Hunt grinned. "You won't get much from now on."

"Huh." Buchanan reflected, reaching for his pants, "Best place for you is right here."

"What about the hotel people?"

"I made such a fuss about havin' this room to myself the Basilios won't come near it. Respect for the law."

"That is very funny," Hunt said. "The law protects me."

"I'll see you get grub and all." He put on his socks, pants and a clean shirt. He struggled into his boots and reached for his hat. His holster and belt hung on a hook, and his rifle was leaning in a corner of the room.

"You goin' out there naked?" Hunt asked.

"Only way to go. This here's a fun crowd. Aggravate 'em, and there could be a foofooraw would harelip the entire State of Texas. Come to think of it, if Major Jones hears about me refereein' the fight, it'll be the same."

"Trouble with you," Hunt said, "it never seems to enter your skull that somebody might take a notion to pick you off."

"Could've been done any time. Reckon they got reasons for wantin' me alive right now."

"Me, too. Otherwise there I was, a sittin' duck for the galoot that killed Masters. A duck in a cage, at that."

"Uh-huh. Killing with reason, that's the whole show. Think on it, Hunt."

"I'm thinkin' . . . what about my horse?"

"Would he head for Lazy M?"

"No. He's my own horse. He'll graze 'til I find him."

"Okay. I'll take care of him. Main thing is, people got to believe you're on the run."

Hunt put a hand to his throat. "One thing always had me worried . . . a rope."

"Don't worry. It'll probably be a bullet, fella like you. You stay put, now, you hear me?"

"Oh, I'm gettin' used to bein' in bed alone," Hunt said. "You know, Buchanan — Masters wasn't such a bad *hombre*."

"He was in the wrong job. It got too big for him. Fella like him, he's a target when things get tight."

"You're a pretty big target your ownself."

"Worried that somebody might get to me before you do?"

"Nope. Truth to tell, I'm goin' to purely hate to kill you," Hunt said.

"Don't let it getcha down," Buchanan said. "Just stick around, and we'll see what we can see."

He took the key with him, locking the door from the outside. He did not want the

Basilios to intrude, and he wanted to keep Hunt honest. If the gunman crawled out the window and took his chances without a horse, that was one thing; to let him prowl the halls of the hotel was another.

He walked through the crowds of merry-makers to the stable. Evidently, no one had discovered Masters, and dead men needed no immediate attention. He moved in the clutter of the stable, found the ladder and climbed it. He made a shushing sound to Coco, who was awake and brooding, as usual.

"Come on down," he whispered. "There's trouble."

"Shootin' trouble, I bet."

"You win."

Coco came down and Buchanan asked, "Where's Bondi?"

"That man goes into the cabin, there, and he don't turn on no light, and he never comes out. That man's crazy or somethin'. He not only don't hear, he don't talk."

Buchanan said, "Help me saddle up Hunt's horse." While they worked in the blackness, making no more sound than necessary, he told Coco what had happened.

Coco said, "This here whole country's gonna die by the gun. This is bad country. I get outa here alive, I'm gonna go to San Francisco."

"Knives," Buchanan said. "They stab you to death in Frisco."

"They get that close, I take my chances."

"You want to take a chance now? You want to take the back way out and ride this horse into the hills and turn him loose? You can run home, get some work thataway."

Coco said, "I don't wanta do it, no."

"I swear Hunt didn't gun down Masters. Somebody tried to get him to escape so it would be blamed on him. If that worked, you could be right about everybody bein' shot down. There would have been a big war right now."

Coco said, "I don't wanta do it. But I'm gonna."

"Okay," Buchanan said. They led out the horse. The noise of revelry was enough to cover their move. "Just turn him loose in the hill country. Loosen his bit so he can graze. Might loosen the cinch, too, just a bit."

"I know what to do," Coco said. "You sure somebody won't shoot at me?"

"Right now, I'm not sure about anything much. I think I'm guessin' good, but that's all."

Coco said, "I'm scared again."

"You do real good when you're scared," Buchanan told him. "I'll come by later to see you."

"Guns," Coco said. "I purely hate guns."

He rode out, taking the long way around.

The whirl of people and noise on the main street were increasing. A big dude with a fancy vest, a diamond ring and a gold nugget watch chain blocked Buchanan's path. He wore a mustache, and his chin was prominent.

"Name of Holloway," he said, flicking ashes from a fat cigar. "Understand you're in charge of the fight."

"You might say." Several less gaudy characters flocked around Holloway, staring at Buchanan.

"I want you to know I got my eye on you. A Ranger runnin' a fight, that don't look too good to me," the big man said. His stomach filled his vest.

Buchanan thought of Coco riding perilously out of town. Any diversion might distract attention.

"You got some notion that it's crooked?" he demanded.

"Me and the boys from Austin," Holloway gestured so that cigar ash fell on Buchanan's boots. "We'll be watchin'. We know the ropes, you better believe."

Buchanan said, "Oh, I believe. I believe in lots of things. One is good manners. You want to step out of my way?"

"I step out of no man's way 'til I get ready!" Holloway roared. "No Ranger who's runnin' an illegal prizefight can tell me nothin'."

People were swirling around. Pat Goodwin came from the hotel. A distraction was one thing, but Buchanan did not hanker for a brawl. He considered a moment, and Holloway stared around. His eyes bulged as prominently as his chin. Buchanan began to take a dislike to the man.

Pat Goodwin was on the edge of the circle of gamblers, who appeared to be backing up Holloway. Vic Carmer came from the saloon and leaned against its wall about where the bullet was imbedded.

Buchanan shrugged. He reached out one long arm and took Holloway by the jaw, pinching tight. With the other hand, he snatched the long cigar. He pushed the cigar into Holloway's vest pocket. He ran the big man backward into his followers.

Pat Goodwin had a six-shooter in his hand. "Steady, there, you people."

They whirled around, and Carmer called a warning. In a jiffy the fight had been prevented. Buchanan spun Holloway and got him by the nape of the neck and the seat of his trousers, turkey-walking him. He beckoned Pat with a nod. This was working well, he thought.

Holloway was bawling like a muley calf under a barbed wire fence, but Buchanan walked him right to the jail. Pat opened the door to the office and stepped inside. Masters lay in congealed blood.

Pat said, "My God, Tom, look at that!"

Buchanan propelled Holloway against the wall, where the big gambler dabbed at his smoking vest in panic. "Somebody got Fred. In the back, too. Better get Doc Gill right now."

He opened the big door to the cells. He picked up a pan of water from the table inside and threw it on Holloway's fancy vest.

"I asked you to step out of the way," he said mildly. "Now you're a coroner's witness besides a public nuisance. There's an open cell down there, I see."

Holloway, his bombast gone, staggered down the cell block. Buchanan said, "There should be a prisoner in there. Keep that in mind when people ask questions, now won't you?"

Holloway managed to say, "Yes, sir. If you say so."

"Good man," Buchanan said. Funny, he thought, how the big, important city boys cooled off when they saw a brass tack. He went back to the office and looked at Masters. It was a shame, all right. Anybody who'd kill a simple soul like the sheriff was a bad customer. There wasn't any reason for such a thing except to start trouble elsewhere. There hadn't been any real reasons for killing Buster or Gabe, either —

except to start a war in the county.

Now if this person or persons had a real reason, such as the upcoming prizefight or the fact that Buchanan was the only law within a hundred miles or so, it would be a very touchy situation. In his long and varied career he had known a Pinkerton detective. The fellow had put his head to work on a problem, and just by thinking he had come up with the answer.

Well, at least they hanged a man for murder on the evidence presented by the detective. Buchanan supposed the man was guilty. He wished the Pinkerton were right there to do some heavy thinking. He thought he might be able to provide a hint or two. Not the real killer, just a lead on him.

Doc Gill came in with Banker Owens and Vic Carmer, these being the most prominent public citizens now. They all stared at Fred Masters as though they didn't believe it was, indeed, him.

Buchanan said, "Backshootin' seems to be the rule around here. Anybody got any ideas?"

"What about Hunt?" Pat asked.

"I looked. He ain't hereabouts," Buchanan said.

"Then he did it!"

"No," Buchanan said. "He was locked up."

"Somebody turned him loose. Maybe Fred brought him out here and he got his gun — is his gun here?"

"His gun is gone. He's gone. Way I figure it, somebody killed Fred, then threw the key in where Hunt could grab it. What would you do, wait for the lynch mob?"

Pat said, "His horse — in the livery stable."

Carmer said, "If he got to his horse, he's gone. Far gone, I should imagine."

"He's guilty," Banker Owens said. "I don't buy that dream of yours, Buchanan. Hunt killed him and vamoosed."

Buchanan looked at Pat. "You believe it?"

Pat said slowly, "Hunt's no backshooter. I don't know. I think we ought to try and find him."

"You want to get a posse together with the fight comin' up tomorrow?" Buchanan asked, "I wish you luck."

Banker Owens said, "Better take Fred to the undertaker. The fight's gotta go on."

Carmer asked, "Shall I check on Hunt's horse for you, Buchanan?"

"You do that." He watched Carmer go out the door.

Doc Gill said, "Fred's been dead for some time."

"Has he?"

"Seems like Hunt could be far away by now."

"Uh-huh," Buchanan said blandly. "Reckon the banker's right. The fight must go on."

"Whoever shot Fred wasn't close to him," the doctor said. "There are no powder marks."

"You couldn't guess what kinda gun was used?"

"It wasn't the same as the one used on Gabe. Not as powerful."

"Could've been a six-shooter?"

"That's my guess. I get to see a heap of gunshot wounds. I'd say a .45."

"Dig it out for me, Doc," Buchanan said. "Take care of Fred, will you? I put a tinhorn in Hunt's cell. He won't need any watchin'. I want to look around."

Pat asked, "Can I do anything?"

"Send Linda home," Buchanan said. "Have her tell what happened." He walked outside with the young man. When they were alone he continued, "Hunt didn't do it. I turned him aloose."

"You did what?" Pat was astounded. "You mean you knew Fred was dead before just now?"

"Yeah. Figure it out. What will Mary do if word gets to her that Hunt did it?"

"She'll have a lynch mob together in jig time. I can't stop her, Tom. There's no way I can figure to stop her."

"Right. No way at all. So I turned him

aloose. Best thing is, the town's all het up about tomorrow."

"But who's doing all this killing?"

"Well, it ain't you. Nor McKay."

"That's what I keep telling Mary."

"So it's got to be somebody else. Somebody with a real reason for startin' a war. Somebody who'd take over both ranches and maybe the town. Somebody right smart."

Pat said, "There's only one somebody fits that description. And he couldn't have done it. He's been around in plain sight whenever anything happened."

Buchanan said, "That's just it."

"Just what?"

"Somebody manages always to be in plain sight — but he's got all the reasons for makin' profit — I choose him."

"But — Mary's in love with him!"

"Yeah, how about that?"

They went up the steps and into the hotel lobby. It was cluttered with odds and ends of people come to the prizefight. Pat was thoughtful.

"I'll tell Linda," he said. "Carmer must be real smart, Tom. What about tomorrow?"

"Yeah. Think on it, Pat. Lazy M will be there. Your sister and her gunnies'll be there. Carmer will be there. You think on that."

"I bet all my cash on Coco. You can believe I'll be there."

"Sure. But think on it."

"Okay."

They parted, Buchanan went up to his room and let himself in. Hunt was sitting on the chair, hands behind his head, without a trace of alarm.

He said, "I watched your little rangdoodle down there. Holloway's got drag in Austin. He owns a congressman. Reckon you won't be a Ranger much longer."

"After tomorrow I won't care," Buchanan said. "You been thinkin' any?"

"What do you think I am, dumb? Might take me a bit of time, but I can see through the hole in a millstone."

"How do you figure it?"

"It was a smart play. Get rid of me, start a war. Whoever gets rubbed out — Carmer don't worry none. He only has to worry about Mary Goodwin."

"Okay. Now I'm goin' to ask one more question. How do you stand?"

"Thought that one out, too. I draw wages from McKay. You and me, that's personal. Whatever you say."

"I say we don't spend the night in this room," Buchanan said. "Couldn't sleep nohow."

"Me neither."

"The Basilios and me, we get along,"

Buchanan said. "It's already slowin' down out there. We better get goin'."

They strapped on their holsters. Buchanan picked up the rifle and handed it to Hunt.

"You better go the back way this time. Meet me at the livery stable."

Hunt looked down at Buchanan's long gun. "One thing about you."

"Lots of things about me," Buchanan said. "You don't know the half of 'em."

"When you trust a man, you trust him all the way."

"Now what would you do with that rifle? Where would you go? What tarnation good would it do you or anybody else? I figure you for a fella with some good sense, maybe more than a lot of other folks hereabouts."

Hunt grinned. "Another thing about you."

"I don't want to hear it." Buchanan's mind was for once, disturbed. The pressure was mounting, and, he knew tomorrow would be a touchy thing. He had never been more concerned about anything than he was now about the prizefight. There were too many openings, too many ways for the killers to move.

"You appreciate a good man when you meet one," Hunt said smugly. "Lead on. See you in the stable."

"And keep it quiet. If Coco comes home

unexpected, he might crown you king of the night."

"I don't aim to fool with Coco none," Hunt said.

They went down the stairs. Maria Basilio's eyes were like saucers when she saw them, but her mouth was shut tight, and Hunt slipped out the rear door while Buchanan went through the lobby and down the street to Carmer's saloon.

Carmer was waiting for him. "Hunt's horse is gone. That settles it. He's guilty."

"You think so?"

"He ran. It's a confession of guilt."

"You a lawyer, Vic?"

"I know a bit of law. A court would consider his flight an indication of guilt."

"You want to raise a posse?"

"There's a fortune bet on the fight." Carmer smiled, shrugging. "I'm not a lawman. And I'd hate to lose out for tomorrow. I imagine Hunt will go to the Lazy M. He can be found, perhaps."

"How about Miss Mary?"

"Really, Buchanan, I can't be altogether responsible for the lady."

"If she knew about Masters, she and her men would be ridin' for the Lazy M." Buchanan shook his head. "They don't give a hoot about the fight."

"I hope no one informs her," Carmer said.

"You and me," Buchanan said. "I got to

be out there early to arrange things."

He went down to the telegraph office. Jackson had no news from Major Jones, which was probably all for the best, Buchanan thought. He went, circuitously, toward the livery stable. He tried to melt his bulk into the shadows. Something or someone scurried, making little noise, going around the back of the stable. He followed, but there was no one in view. He went to the cabin where Bondi lived, but it was shut tight, dark as the moonless night.

Then he heard an almost soundless struggle taking place inside the stable. He ran as fast as he could, and there were two forms rolling around in the clutter. He grabbed hold, and with all his strength he tore Hunt from Coco. The fighter staggered back into a corner. There was the sound of clanking metal. Buchanan let go of Hunt, jumped and caught a toppling, well-wrapped object.

"Youall hush up," he whispered as loud as he could. "Doggone, you'll spoil everything."

"Guns," Coco said hoarsely. "He's a gun fella."

"He's on our side right now," Buchanan said. "Calm down, will you?"

The object in his hands felt familiar. He motioned them up into the loft and carried it along with him. They hung a blanket over the window through which Coco had stared so many lonely hours. Buchanan began to unwrap the bundle.

Hunt said, “Didn’t mean to scare you, Coco. You come in all hot and feisty.”

“There was something in the yard,” Coco said. “Couldn’t see good enough. They been whisperin’ at me. Then you was there, waitin’, and I thought it was them.”

Buchanan said, “Never mind that. Just looky here.”

Hunt came and stood over him. “That’s there’s a Sharps rifle. Ain’t seen one in a long time now. Best buffalo gun ever was. Hit a flea in the eye at a hundred paces.”

“Makes a loud noise, too.” Buchanan looked up at him.

After a moment, Hunt said, “Yeah. Reckon that’s it.”

“Must be the only one of its kind around. That’s why he left the shells here and there.”

“Uh-huh,” Hunt said. “Could be like that, all right.”

“Oh, it’s like that. Thing is, how we do it now? You and me?”

“Any bullets with it?”

“Plenty.”

“Okay,” Hunt said.

“You know what to do?”

“Guns is my business.”

Coco moaned, “Guns, guns, always guns.”

"You got to make 'em work for you," Hunt explained. He took out his Barlow. "Better get to work before somebody misses this beauty."

Stremple was sweating. The crowd had thinned out in the saloon. There was more interest in the prizefight to be held in the morning than in further wassailing. Carmer sat behind his desk, his fingers tapping, one eye twitching.

"The nigger, Buchanan — *and* Hunt. And Jackson said the nigger bet a hundred on himself. He didn't have a hundred of his own, I swear it. I went through him careful to make sure he wasn't pulling something on us." Stremple held out his hands. They were shaking. "Buchanan almost caught me."

"You can outrun anybody," Carmer said, but his eye continued to twitch.

"True." He had been part of a con which involved a foot race when he met Carmer. "I've done some fancy footwork hereabouts. But this was close."

"Buchanan and the Nigra," Carmer said. "It is too late by far to do anything about that. Everyone and his brother knows Buchanan is the referee, all that. Try and change it, and we'd all be in the fire."

"If he wasn't wearing that damn badge — but he is."

"It'll take some thinking," Carmer said.

"Oliver hasn't been drinking. He's as strong as need be. And the coon must be scared . . . No, I take that back. Coco is not scared. Coco's got Buchanan."

"Something must be done," Carmer said. He wished his eye would not continue to wink like a bat in a windstorm. He had time enough, he told himself. He had not come this far to be foiled by a dumb giant, a Nigra and a gunman.

Dungan came into the office at the Lazy M. Mary Goodwin was sleeping with her arms on the desk, her head buried. The whiskey bottle, uncorked, was at her elbow. Dungan's face twisted. He put the bottle away and stood there, uncertain. Without his hat, it could be seen that his head came to a point, suggesting malfunction at birth. When he went to Mary's side, his oversized spurs jangled and she awakened, looking at him out of her huge dark eyes. There were slight marks of combat on her, which sent shivers down the tiny gunman's spine.

He said, "I'm real sorry, Miss Mary, but I got bad news for you."

"Bad news," she muttered. She looked for the bottle, then recovered herself. She did not drink before others. "What do we ever get but bad news?"

"Like you said, I left Cactus hangin'

around town, keepin' outa sight. Miss Mary, they got the sheriff."

She came erect on the chair, her hands planted on the desk top. "Fred? He was Pa's friend. They killed him?"

"Hunt did it. He got clean away. With the prizefight and everything — nobody did nothin'."

She said, "The prizefight. Yes. Tomorrow."

"We'll have to wait until it's over. Then I'll take the boys and wipe 'em out. Buchanan, the Lazy M, everybody."

"Yes," she said. Now she was herself, fire emanating from her. "We'll wipe the slate clean."

"Uh — the boys want to see the fight. Is that all right?"

"All those people . . . Let me think." She rubbed a hand across her face. "Where's Pat?"

"With, you know, the McKay Gal."

"That slut. Vic — now Pat. Buchanan in between. That bitch." The headache was returning. Where had she put the bottle? Dungan didn't count: Dungan was her slave. She rummaged in the drawer and poured a drink. Then she blinked hard and reached behind her for another four-ounce shot glass and poured one for Dungan. She did not offer any explanation. She drained two ounces of the whiskey. It wasn't as smooth as that her father had left behind.

"What about the fight?"

"Well, I figure from there, when it's over, we start the war. Nobody'll be expectin' it. Holiday and all." His eyes gleamed. "Buchanan the referee up there, a target."

"Yes. I see that." She swallowed. "Vic, what's he doing?"

Dungan said with distaste, "Tendin' his saloon Miss Mary, it ain't none of my business, but that man . . . I don't cotton to that man."

She smiled a whiskey smile. "You wouldn't cotton to any man looks twice at me, now would you, Dungan?"

He turned a fiery red, and the spurs tinkled as he shuffled his feet. "Miss Mary, he ain't our kind of people. He's too slick. And he's a city man."

She said cruelly, "He's my man, Dungan. Don't you ever forget it."

"He carries tales but he ain't helped us one bit," Dungan persisted. "He's just mouthy. This here is a war."

"My man," she repeated. She finished the drink. The headache diminished but would not go away. "When the chips are down, you'll see. He'll be there."

"I got to see it to believe it."

"You'll see. And you'll do what I tell you to do. Pat — he's deserted. He quit the Rangers. I'll run him out of the county. Vic and me, we'll run the show. You'll see."

Defeated easily by her, Dungan lifted one shoulder and said meekly, "Yes, Miss Mary. whatever you say, that's right with me. Better get some sleep now. The fight's in the mornin' and you'll want to be there."

"I'll be there." She would wear male clothing and put her hair beneath her sombrero. "I'll be there with bells on." She would start the war right there. She had to pull herself together and think hard. She poured another drink. "Get your boys ready for anything."

"They're always ready. They good boys."

"Uh-huh." She turned her mind inward. She did not even know when he left the office on tiptoe, the spurs playing a muted tune.

The town was silent. The moon began to peek from behind a black cloud. Tomorrow would be fair, Buchanan thought. He stayed close to the buildings and came to the spot where the bullet had entered the wall of Carmer's saloon. He pried with the slimmest blade of the Barlow. He made quite a hole, but he dug out the bullet which had missed his head. He put it in his pocket. He had found putty in the trash of Bondi's stable, but he debated a moment, then decided to leave the scar for all to see. It was coming close to time, and a silent threat might upset his adversaries.

He walked the short distance to the bank and went into an alley. He used the pocket knife and a small crowbar on a window. He crammed his bulk through the window into the bank and lit a tiny lantern he had also rescued from the stable junk.

He found the ledgers as he had expected, unlocked, roosting on a shelf. Oswald Owens was too much the sport to be over-careful about anything, he had figured. He made certain that his little but sharp lamp did not shine on a window, but he was satisfied that no one would be watching at that early morning hour. He hunkered down, thumbed the alphabet of the deposit book and began counting the fortunes of various Scottsville citizens, one in particular.

CHAPTER TEN

Buchanan was atop the chosen one of the Twin Flats early. The sports were stirring, anxious for the spectacle, and poor Fred Masters lay cold in his coffin.

Pat Goodwin helped test the eight ring posts on which were draped ropes which formed a twenty-four-foot squared circle. The turf was level enough, although not completely smooth. This would favor Oliver Green, the bigger, more powerful contestant.

Pat said, "I like bein' Coco's second all right. But I'll need help if I have to tote him to the corner. He weighs up to a yearlin' bull, that one."

"I'll get help for you. I got to warn you again, it's going to be dangerous right out here in plain sight."

"Since last night I don't feel anything can hurt me, the way it was with Linda before she went home. Nothin' can stop me now, not even a .45 slug."

"Not even your sister?"

"Way I figure, she wants Vic Carmer, let 'em live in town. The GG and Lazy M are goin' to tie in together and stop all this fightin."

"You sure of that?"

"Me and Linda against the world. She's bringin' her daddy this mornin' with the intent to settle it."

"And Mary'll have her gun hands around to start a fight."

"But I got you to prevent it."

Buchanan sighed. "One Texas Ranger against the world. And I ain't even a for-real Ranger."

"I note you're wearin' your gun today."

"But not the badge." Buchanan shook his head. "It's a cock-eyed world sometimes. I'm glad you're talkin' with Scott McKay, because I got a notion."

"About what?"

"You and him both act as seconds to Coco."

Pat said, "Hey, now. That would show the whole county that we're together."

"Yep."

"That's one hiyu notion you got!"

"Uh-huh. Only it'll make Mary's red hair turn purple."

Pat said, "It can't be any worse with her. Nothin' can make it worse. Nothin' can make her believe Lazy M didn't have Pa killed."

"If I can't prove it before the day's over," Buchanan said, "then we'll all wind up in hell."

Pat said, "I been in the Rangers. You beat the bunch of 'em all hollow, Tom."

"Get a man and his gal together, and the whole world looks rosy," Buchanan mused. "Is that Lazy M I see ridin' from the east, there?"

"That's them!" Pat strode down the hill so fast he almost fell.

Buchanan looked over at the other of the Twin Flats. The heavy foliage and the stumpy, thick trees were perfect concealment. He could distinguish no motion except that of a welcome gentle breeze which stirred the fronds, the leaves and the wild flowers.

He looked down into the hollow where the horses would be hobbled for the event and saw Pat offering a hand to help Linda down from a horse. She'd been leaping in and out of saddles only since she was a baby, but it looked like she was suddenly made of glass or something. McKay was shaking hands with Pat. Obie Deal, Madigan, Bender . . . all were there except a couple of unfortunates left behind, by the luck of the draw, to attend the ranch.

Well, he thought, a little talk with a little gal could pay off. Good thing Linda had taken to him from the start. Good thing McKay had appreciated his stand in the matter of Gabe's death. That part had worked out all right. Only trouble was that

Lazy M was no match at all for the forces arrayed against them. They hadn't a chance in hell, and if Buchanan were wrong they might not survive this day, this fine day on a mesa adjacent to the great Texas plains.

Now McKay was nodding agreement with whatever Pat said, and again they shook hands. Then Madigan and Bender mounted up again and rode to town. They would be bringing Coco to the top of the mesa. After a moment, Obie Deal rode after them. Pat was taking no chances on the opposition trying a trick.

Buchanan looked to the west, but as yet there was no sign of the GG Ranch bunch. People were beginning to straggle from town in carriages, afoot and on horseback. Carmer and Stremple had asserted that they would second their man in the ring; they should be along any time now. It was a strange way to have everything come to a boil, he thought, but then his whole life had consisted, thus far, of a series of odd and interesting climaxes. He looked again at the trees on the other mesa and felt a twinge down his spine. He knew that, big as he was, he was a marvelous target.

Danger would be at every point — there was no avoiding it. He had made his plans but, even in so doing, had known that he was marked. He was now certain of the killer and the motive behind the murders, but he had no real proof. His only chance was to bring everything into the open, to lance the boil on Scottsville's neck. It could be nothing but painful. The question was, who would suffer the most and who would prevail?

Linda McKay and her father came up the hill. The rancher offered his hand — it was his day for handshaking, it seemed. Linda tilted her head to look up at him and offered a cheek to be kissed.

McKay said, "I been lots of kinds of a damn fool. You have done a great job, Buchanan."

"So far, so good," Buchanan said. "I don't like the way it is. Linda told you?"

"Linda and Pat. Looks like I have myself a son-in-law there. I guess that's thanks to you, also."

"You can bet on that," Linda said. "Pat grew up overnight. Tom had a lot to do with it."

"No," Buchanan said. "You can't grow up another man. Pat came to face himself and saw what he was and what he wanted to be. It was always in him, he's Gabe's son as much as anything. Reckon he got some of the best of both of his parents."

Pat finished seeing to the horses and waved to them. He was too young to be in this mess, Buchanan thought, but he'd be all right if he survived. He watched the young man approach.

McKay was saying, "Far as Pat and I are concerned, the trouble between the ranches is over. What about Mary?"

"Yeah," Buchanan said. "I couldn't know what about her no way. I only know I feel right sorry for her."

"If her men start something in this crowd, it will be a massacre," McKay said. He was sober-faced but not afraid.

"I'll do anything I can," Buchanan promised.

"I know you've got plans. I won't ask what they are." McKay paused. "I'm disappointed in Hunt . . . Running away like that. I figured he'd stick, and we could use him today."

"Don't fret about Hunt," Buchanan said. "Just keep your guns handy and wait it out."

"There's nothing else to do. I tried to make Linda stay away — no chance."

She had gone to Pat, and they were whispering and laughing together as though there wasn't a care in the world. Buchanan hunched a huge shoulder.

"Love in a tub — and the bottom fell out. That's what my father used to say. But it's real nice to see young people like that."

Now the crowd was descending on the plain like a plague of locusts. A carriage broke loose and came briskly ahead. In it were Oliver Green, Stremple and Carmer.

McKay said, "I sure thought Linda was making a dead set for you, Buchanan."

"Some gals have to know there's an admirer around. They got their own strength, but a man makes 'em feel more womanly, seems like. I enjoyed Linda. She's one fine little gal."

The sun was up bright, but there was a breeze from the mountain range to the north. There would be room on the mesa for them all, but it would be crowded. He didn't like that part of it.

The Lazy M boys were coming in the near distance with Coco mounted on a livery horse and wrapped in a Navajo blanket of bright hues. Cowboys were riding the flat in circles and whooping, in their fashion. The gamblers mainly came afoot, making last-minute wagers. It was an exciting scene, one which Buchanan ordinarily would have enjoyed to the hilt. Today the feeling of danger was ever present.

It was not his own skin he was worried about; it was the fact that, if he did not act correctly at the proper instant, there would be blood shed atop the Twin Flat, the blood of innocent people.

Now he saw the GG Ranch bunch coming across from the west. Mary Goodwin's ample curves could not be disguised by the men's clothing she wore. Dungan was a mite aboard a big horse. The hard-faced gunmen threw black shadows as they rode that seemed blacker than those cast by others.

The carriage bearing Oliver Green veered. The GG people rode to it and formed a bodyguard for it as they came to the base of the mesa. The Lazy M men escorting Coco made the same maneuver in the east.

McKay said fretfully, "Without Hunt, my boys can't handle those killers with Mary Goodwin. I hope you know what you're doing, Buchanan."

"You better do more'n hope," Buchanan told him. "You better pray a little."

It was time to climb into the ring. From now until the fight ended, he would be in complete command. He would decide the winner and bestow the bag of gold. On his head was the responsibility.

The people were thronging to the site. Banker Owens carried a recognizable canvas sack shirred with a string in which was the cash prize — two hundred dollars. He managed to get tangled in the ropes, and Buchanan extricated him, the town rich man suffering some loss of dignity.

Coco entered the ring with Pat Goodwin and Scott McKay. He was sweating under the blanket, which was a sign of being in good condition, Buchanan thought. His eyes rolled.

"Guns," he said. "Too many guns. Even you."

"Just be glad you found that gun in the stable," Buchanan said. "You feel all right?"

"What about the whisperer? What about I lay down to him?"

Buchanan said, "Forget it."

"How'm I goin' to forget it?"

"Just fight your fight."

"I got no other way."

"You'll get a square deal."

"I need more'n that, somethin' tells me."

Across the ring, Oliver Green, Stremple and Carmer had taken their places. Banker Owens came to the forefront and made a speech, about the great sports of Scottsville and the manly art of prizefighting, to which no one really listened. Buchanan waited patiently until the last straggler had made his way up the hill and had found a vantage point. He took one more look at the other Flats peak. Then he thought over the salient points of the London Prize Ring rules that should be made clear before the start of the match. He went to ring center. Banker Owens toted the bag of cash to a spot that was neutral but excellent for viewing the proceedings. Buchanan raised a hand for silence and got it. He could see Mary Goodwin and the GG Ranch crowd behind Green's corner. The girl's eyes were big as saucers, staring at him, going to

Carmer and softening, then moving to her brother across the way. They narrowed and hardened when she saw the McKays at Coco's back.

Now Oliver Green and Coco stood in their corners, recognizing the referee. Green removed a lightweight shirt to reveal his brawn. Coco wore professional tights with an American flag tucked into the belt. Green wore winter longjohns of deep red. Both men wore soft shoes, although spikes not exceeding three-eighths of an inch were legal.

Buchanan took a sharp stick from his belt and made a deep scratch exactly at ring center. The crowd watched and listened. Many of them had never seen a prize fight before. Those who had were curious as to Buchanan's knowledge of the game.

He looked at Green's corner, and Carmer announced loudly, "My man is ready."

Pat Goodwin responded, "Our man is ready."

Buchanan said, "This professional match is to be held under the London Prize Ring rules. Come to center ring, please."

The two men were a striking contrast. The towering Green was as tall as Buchanan and roped with muscles, an overnight beard giving him a menacing appearance, his skin white as marble. The shorter black man, with his ivory teeth and steady brown eyes, was poised and lithe, the picture of a trained athlete.

Buchanan examined them, especially their belts, where certain fighters had been known to store metal, stones or other improper substances, such as snuff or red pepper for an opponent's eyes. Finding nothing, he addressed the adversaries.

"Each fighter'll come to the mark at the call of time." He indicated the mark he had made in the earth. "When I call it, time shall be in and the round commence, the fighter rising from the knee of his second and coming forward. A round shall end when one or both contestants is down."

Carmer called, "About the wrestling . . ."

There was a sound of "Hush!" Buchanan, not even looking at Green's corner, continued:

"A man is down when his knee hits the ground. There will be no falling without being hit. Rasslin' holds will be allowed. Anything goes but gougin', bitin', kickin' the opponent. Violations will be decided by the referee, and if a man fouls he forfeits the fight and the purse."

He looked over at the other Twin Flat and let his words sink in for a moment.

"There will be no buttin' with the head. No hittin' a man when he's down. No hittin' below the belt. No stranglin' a man caught in the ropes. Now, at the end of a round a

man has thirty seconds to get ready to fight again. Thirty seconds . . . Then I will count to eight, and if he is not at the mark at the end of that count — he loses the bout. There'll be no recount. The referee is the last resort. Understand?"

The fighters nodded. A roar went up from the crowd. They wanted action now; there had been enough words. Buchanan motioned the contestants back to their corners. Pat Goodwin made a knee for Coco to perch on. On the other side, Green did not deign to seat himself.

The suspense mounted. Buchanan thrust his little stick in the ground against a ring post, where it would be handy for restoring the mark before each round. He let the crowd wait for a moment. Then he said with solemn dignity, "Gentlemen, you will please come to the mark."

They came and stood straight. Green loomed above the black man. Coco offered his hand.

Green took the hand and applied pressure, twisting. Buchanan came in like a flash. He took Green by the elbow and collar and pinched with his huge fingers. Green howled in pain and let go of Coco.

Buchanan hurled Green away from him and roared, "One more foul on the part of this man, and the match will be forfeited."

Carmer leaped up and cried, "Oliver

thought the match had begun. He didn't mean to foul."

"He hurt me," Green was moaning. "The referee is on that nigger's side!"

Buchanan waved to Dr. Gill, who came into the ring. The local people recognized the respected physician and drowned the cries from others suspicious of the occurrence and its possible effects.

Doc Gill said, "No harm done. The man is able to continue."

"Toe the mark," Buchanan barked before further furor could occur.

Green returned to his place, glaring. Coco faced him.

"Time!"

The orthodox prizefighter, Coco danced, left fist extended, palm turned upward, right hand cocked on his chest. Green set himself, crouching. As Coco led a left, Green again grabbed and caught the left wrist of the black man.

He was better than had been believed, Buchanan thought. Green was an accomplished wrestler; it was plain to be seen by his use of leverage. It had long been granted that a good wrestler could nine times out of ten defeat a good boxer at even weights. Poor Coco was in for it.

Green applied his strength and tried for a hammerlock. Coco could not break loose. His punches had no effect. Green got the arm up in the small of Coco's back and ran with him, using him as a human battering ram.

Coco's head struck a ring post. The ropes collapsed. The crowd hooted. Carmer was on his feet, fists clenched. Mary Goodwin stood at his elbow, jumping with glee.

Buchanan pushed Green away from the prone Coco, calling, "Time, end of Round One."

Pat and McKay ran to pick up Coco. They lugged him to the corner. Willing hands righted the ring post and tightened the ropes. Buchanan grimly kept his eyes on his railroad watch.

There was a trickle of blood from Coco's ear. He was dazed. The Lazy M men were ready with a water bucket and a huge sponge, but Coco shook them off as he strove to regain reason.

The thirty seconds ran away, and Buchanan was forced to call time. Green rushed out. Buchanan had to stop him at the mark with one hand while he began to toll off eight seconds with the other. Coco came awake all at once, it seemed, and trotted to position.

Green sought the Greco-Roman hold and tried a trip with his left heel. Coco seemed to fall into the trap, going limp. Green threw him again.

Coco did not go down. He circled. When

Green came within the circle's circumference, Coco struck out. Moving inside the long arms of the white man, he threw short, heavy blows. One landed on Green's nose, and he squealed like a pig under a fence. Another clipped his right eye.

Then Green wrapped one arm around Coco's neck and began beating him with flailing wallops on the kidneys, on the nape of the neck and on the middle of his back. Coco squirmed like an eel and broke the hold. They stood a moment, a study in contrast, straining against each other. Then Green used his enormous strength and sent Coco reeling and stumbling to his knees. That was the end of Round Two.

Green was bleeding from the nose, and his eye was puffed. Coco took deep breaths, not listening to the excited, nonprofessional advice of his seconds, his deepset eyes dark and dangerous with growing fury. Buchanan kept the time and called them back to action.

Green knew one way to fight: to get hold of the smaller man and maul him. His hands clawed out, but Coco was not there; he was dancing backwards, fists high, parrying. He was catlike now, quick and sharp. His hard fists beat against Green's face and ribs. His sweaty body helped him slide out of attempted embraces. Green went off-balance, and now Coco came in, belted hard to the body — then turned his hip and executed the schoolboy trip. Now it was Green who went tumbling. He fell full length.

Bettors upon Coco screamed their approval. He walked to his corner straight and proud. But he had met a man who was obviously a skilled and trained wrestler. This was no mere strong boy and part-time smithy. Carmer had set the scene for a killing with some skill, Buchanan thought.

They were working on Green with all sorts of medication. Stremple and Carmer had lied about their knowledge of the game. They were talking to him, urging him on. He was a veteran, and he seemed game enough. It was an even match thus far.

The two came out for the next round. Green sought the wrist hold which had been successful before. Coco rapped with his fist on the forearm of the bigger man, and Buchanan suppressed a chuckle, remembering how he had used the same trick back in El Paso on first meeting the prizefighter. Green pulled back.

Coco was in on him with a shrewd left and a whopping right fist. Coco moved away. Green followed, seeking to get in close. Coco retreated in high style, flicking out with his fists, sometimes to the muscles in the long arms, sometimes to the eye and nose.

Stremple yelled, "Make that nigger stand up and fight."

Coco's backers hooted, "Rassler, Green's a rassler!"

Green was indeed a wrestler. He cornered Coco on the ropes and seized him in a bearlike grip. He sunk his chin into the dark shoulder and essayed to break Coco's back.

Coco spun around. Big as he was, Green had to go with him. Coco shook himself like a spaniel coming out of water. Green flew off at a tangent. Coco followed.

Green came all the way around with both fists. It was a double pivot punch. He struck Coco in the head and knocked him flat. Buchanan leaned in and beckoned to Pat and McKay to come and get their man.

It seemed now that Coco would never recover in time. Green, bleeding, one eye almost closed, stood inhaling deep breaths, his hands opening and closing, ready for the kill, if necessary. Carmer and Stremple were smiling. Mary Goodwin's eyes were wild and triumphant. The Lazy M gunmen hunched in close behind Dungan in back of Green's corner.

Pat Goodwin pulled the cork on a bottle of ammonia and held it under Coco's nose as Buchanan had instructed him. McKay rubbed the back of his neck. Coco's eyes did not open. Buchanan began to worry.

There was nothing to do but call "Time." Green came confidently to the mark.

Coco barely managed to get to his feet. He staggered. Buchanan had called, "Seven . . . and" when he made it to the mark, a pitiful object, an easy prey.

Green reached out two big hands to take Coco's head and twist it. The fight seemed all over.

Coco ducked. Green grabbed at empty air. Coco, throwing punches from a crouch, sunk ringing hooks into Green's body.

Coco, Buchanan suddenly realized, had been faking. Coco was a professional also, using his own guile against the skills of a superior wrestler.

Green doubled over, his face gone white. Coco deliberately hit him on the injured eye and on the nose. Green tried to escape. Coco's swift legs, strengthened on the long, lonely runs, carried him ahead. Green tried to hang on.

Coco shoved him away, again and again he slammed to the midriff until Buchanan ached with the rhythm of the blows. The crowd was in a frenzy.

Buchanan, facing the other Twin Flat, lifted his hand in a signal. A man unnoticed by the crowd occupied with the fight answered him and knelt among the Lazy M horses, looked eastward, then rode swiftly around the base of the mesa to the west.

Green swung wildly with both hands. Coco hit him on the side of the jaw. Green swayed like an oak under the ax of a woodsman. Coco hit him on the chin.

Green fell on his face. Stremple and Carmer rushed to get him to drag him to the corner. They could not bring him erect. All their devices failing, Stremple struck a match and attempted to apply it to Green's body. Buchanan strode, watch in hand, to Green's corner and slapped the flame away from the already tortured man.

". . . And eight," he yelled above the crowd's sound. "The winner of this match is . . . Coco Bean!"

Mary Goodwin's eyes flamed. She turned to Dungan. The gunmen reached for their holsters. Now was the moment of fear as Buchanan turned and saw the Lazy M men presenting a solid front, weapons in hand. In a moment the war would be on. People near either of the factions bellowed and fought to get down from the mesa, tumbling over one another. There was the far-off booming sound of a big gun. Smoke rose from a tree on the other Twin Flat.

Buchanan drew his six-gun and stood in ring center. "Just hold it, everybody."

From behind the Lazy M crowd a familiar voice drawled, "You heard the man."

Dungan squealed, "Hunt, you bastard!" and wheeled around with both guns drawn.

Stremple and Carmer fell away. The other GG Ranch men kept one eye on Buchanan and did not move a muscle.

Hunt laughed and fired one time.

Dungan went backwards as though hit by a cannonball. He struck against the ropes of the ring and rebound. He coughed, and his guns fell to earth. Then he collapsed into a tiny heap of clothing and hat.

Buchanan said, "Easy does it."

The Lazy M bunch held their guns steady. Mary Goodwin, looking around wildly, saw that she had no support. She ran for the edge of the mesa and down the hill toward her horse. Pat and Obie Deal cut across the flat and pursued her.

Buchanan said, "You, there. Cactus, Jorey, Montana. Drop your belts."

With Mary and Dungan gone, they had no stomach for a fight. They obeyed.

Carmer and Stremple were staring, uncomfortable and undecided. Oliver Green bled a lot.

Buchanan said, "Better get your man to town, hadn't you, Vic? Doc will have his hands full with Mary Goodwin for a while. Oliver looks like he don't feel well."

"You're right, Buchanan," Carmer said. He looked at Coco. "Congratulations. You're a fine fighter."

Coco said, "Scared. I'm a scared fighter."

With some difficulty, Carmer and Stremple got Green to his feet and steered him down to where the carriage waited. Hunt was getting impatient, holding down the imported gunmen.

"Hey, Buchanan. What about these ducks? You think we oughta do somethin' for 'em?"

"Let them do somethin' for the community," Buchanan said. "Let 'em tote Dungan to the undertaker's."

"Now, that is what I call a notion," Hunt said. He had never seemed so blithe. "You heard him, you rannies. Tote!"

"Put 'em in your hangout," Buchanan said. "You can split your mattresses with 'em."

There were still people hanging around, notably Oswald Owens, who was still shaking in his congress gaiters but smiling weakly at the thought of his winnings. He began to orate, but Buchanan stopped him.

"The day's not over. There'll be some answers to questions we been askin' about Gabe Goodwin. Better get the people back to town."

He hefted the meager purse and tossed it to Coco. Down below, he saw Pat and Obie Deal catch up to Mary. They walked her between them, where she moved like a big doll, stifflegged. The death of Dungan so close at hand must have shocked her, he thought.

Coco said, "Oliver thought I was goin' to take the dive. He kept askin' me in close. He kept sayin', 'Nigger, you better fall down or a bullet'll gitcha'. It was scary."

"His boss forgot to tell him the deal was off," Buchanan said. "They knew it. They put us together last night."

"How you know that?" Coco demanded.

"The shadow in the stable yard," Buchanan told him. "And other things. Like a hole in Carmer's wall."

"I think you crazy," Coco said, clutching his purse. "But we're alive. Yessir, we're still alive."

Linda McKay and her father came to stand close to Coco. "It worked," McKay said.

"Thanks to Hunt," Buchanan said. "Could've been a lot of people hurt if he didn't time it out just right."

"What about that shot from over yonder?"

"We were lookin' for that."

"I didn't hear the sound of a bullet."

"If you did — I wouldn't be here talkin' with you," Buchanan said. "Maybe Coco wouldn't, either . . . if he had time to reload that Sharps."

McKay said, "I don't understand all of it. But you handled this crowd fine."

"One mob — one Ranger." Buchanan grinned. "Maybe you better bring your boys into town for the finish. Maybe a few surprises yet."

"I wouldn't miss it for the world," Linda McKay said. "I hope it's not too tough on poor Mary. She's sick. I've believed she was sick for some time now."

"I'm sorry about Mary, too," Buchanan said. "But then, I been sorry about Gabe and Buster, the cook, and a whole lot of things."

CHAPTER ELEVEN

Buchanan made the sheriff's office headquarters, for the moment. Holloway, the big gambler, departed with mixed emotions as a winner who had not been allowed to witness the fight. The three imported GG gunmen sulked in the cells. Hunt lounged, and Coco, refreshed by a bath and wearing his clean Levis, boots and hat, was like new.

Hunt said, "I don't know. This here is all cock-eyed for me."

"Who else could be sheriff?"

"It ain't right," Hunt said. "I feel all backward."

"McKay is for it. The banker is for it. They're goin' to hold an election soon as the mess is cleaned up."

"Me, a lawman." But Hunt was secretly as pleased as he was amazed.

"You saved the bacon up on the mesa," Buchanan told him. "And we ain't out of the woods yet."

Coco mourned, "More gun shootin'."

Doc Gill came in. "Mary won't listen to me. I gave her a sedative, but I couldn't get through to her."

"She at the hotel?" Buchanan asked.

"Yes. People are decamping in droves. In an hour, there won't be an outlander in Scottsville."

"Guns," Coco said. "Folks don't like guns goin' off."

Buchanan said to Dr. Gill, "It'll be a crowded inquest. Any law against holdin' it at the livery stable?"

"Why, no," Dr. Gill said. "I've held them in saloons."

"Outdoors in the yard at the livery," Buchanan said. "In an hour or so?"

"We didn't hold an inquest for Fred Masters as yet."

"Figured we'd have 'em both at once."

The physician was thoughtful. "I think I understand. Have you made plans?"

"Near as I could," Buchanan said. "We been lucky so far."

"I'll be there." Dr. Gill departed.

Coco said, "That Jackson, he was scared when he paid off the bet. Carmer and them are all huddled up in the saloon. Only Bondi, he forkin' manure like every day."

Buchanan said, "The McKays will want to be at the inquest. There'll be others."

"Just about everybody," Hunt agreed. "It's tetchy."

"Banker Owens. See that he gets there, Hunt."

"Hey, I ain't a lawman yet."

"You can act like one. Practice, Hunt, practice," Buchanan said.

He had an hour to think it over. He sat behind the sheriff's desk with only Coco for company and talked it out as the prize-fighter sat nodding, his brown eyes bright.

Vic Carmer sat behind his desk in his office. The saloon was almost deserted. Jackson was tending bar, leaving the telegraph office unattended. He started at every small sound, his face greenish with fear.

"Buchanan knew — he knew everything," Carmer said. "But how? How did he find out?"

"The nigger," Stremple said bitterly. "He and the nigger were together all the time."

"That part we know."

Oliver Green, bandaged and hunched in a corner, said, "You never told me the nigger wouldn't quit to me."

"We told you to fight your best," Carmer said sharply. "Why destroy your confidence by telling you the fix was off? You might have been hurt worse than you are."

"I'd be dead if I was," Green complained.

"If we could only get out of the country," Stremple said.

"Without money? With the telegraph wires running to every hick town? With the Rangers after us?" Carmer shrugged. "No, it's not over here as yet. I talked to Mary just now, at the hotel."

"Her brother came to life," Stremple said. "Lazy M and GG are together now."

"Let Buchanan show his proof of anything," Carmer said. "He might make a lot of guesses, but where's his proof?"

"He goes to the gun if he has to. For a peaceable man, he can sure raise a ruckus."

Green muttered, "He gets his hands on you, he don't need a gun. I felt his strength there in the ring."

Carmer sat back. What would Uncle Horace do in such a spot, he wondered? The answer was plain: Uncle Horace would not have put himself in this particular predicament. Only the widow had caught Horace Carmer without a safe avenue of retreat. It had been such a sure thing, so easy before Buchanan had lumbered into it.

Now it came down to another woman, but a vastly different woman, he thought, his hopes rising. She had faked taking the medicine the doctor gave her. She was full of thoughts of vengeance — and of the whiskey she had demanded.

He took off his coat. He found an old weapon in the drawer and arranged it with a string so that it pointed down his right sleeve. He dangled another over-and-under .50 caliber derringer in the cuff, where it was convenient to his left hand but concealed by the sleeve. He put the coat back on. He was not a man accustomed to killing, but he knew all the devious ways in which it could be committed.

He was rather proud of himself. He knew it would be a close call, and he knew the penalty involved, but he was calm. His eyelid did not blink, now that the last chips were down.

He said "Stremple, you've always had nerve. Oliver, you're a tough man. If we play it right we can come out of this. All we need is to buy some time."

"But we haven't got getaway money," Stremple said.

"The bank is loaded with it today," Carmer reminded him. "If we can manage the time we can crack it."

Stremple brightened. "Say, I hadn't thought of that."

"Just do your job and leave the thinking to me," Carmer said. "I don't like it any more than you do. I don't like it about the livery stable. But we might as well get at it."

He rose. It had been a good time in Scottsville, and his plans had been solid, he thought. He was a prominent citizen, and he was engaged to be married to a cattle queen — of sorts. He might well have made it all — if it weren't for that damned Buchanan.

If it's the last thing I do, he told himself, I'll kill that big yokel.

The coroner's jury sat uncomfortable on a plank which rested on two nail kegs from the cluttered livery stable. Bondi never stopped forking the manure into the pit, oblivious to the proceedings. He was a skinny man who could get lost in a crowd of three. McKay, Owens, Obie Deal and Pat Goodwin, along with Basilio from the hotel, made up the panel.

Dr. Gill said, "It is the decision of the jury that Edward Dungan met his death at the hands of Sylvester Hunt, who fired in self-defense."

Buchanan rolled his eyes at Hunt and mouthed, "Sylvester?" He got a glare in exchange.

"However," Dr. Gill continued, "Ranger Buchanan has requested that the cases of Buster Delehanty and Gabriel Goodwill, both of whom died at the hands of a person or persons unknown, be here reopened. Request is granted."

Carmer, Stremple and Oliver were spread out among the spectators, all townspeople. Buchanan took position where he could keep them within his view. Hunt leaned against the wall of the barn, hipshot, seemingly indifferent.

Mary Goodwin was not present, nor were

the other GG riders. The gunmen were in the jail. It seemed a good arrangement.

Buchanan said, "Thing is, I learned some facts." He produced several small items. "These bullets, now. The brass shells, they were left behind when Buster and Gabe were killed and when someone took a shot at either me or Pat Goodwin . . . Now, this hunk of lead here, it was taken from Gabe's body."

He placed the objects on a barrel head. He put another misshapen hunk of lead beside them. "And this was taken from the front of Carmer's saloon — where it landed after missing me or Pat. And this one — it was taken from the body of Fred Masters . . . it don't match the other lead, it's from a .45. Sounds like a big mix-up, don't it?"

Nobody offered comment.

"Now there is evidence," Buchanan continued, "that when the shot was fired that killed Gabe — and also the one that missed me — that the sound of the gun was loud. A booming sound."

Coco appeared in the door of the stable. He gingerly held the Sharps rifle. He put it across the barrel head and retreated.

Buchanan said, "Youall know how a Sharps sounds. Now, this mornin' at the end of the fight we all heard the same sound. Only this time there was no bullet to kill anybody. Hunt?"

Hunt spoke without moving. "We found that gun in the stable. I pried the lead out of the cartridges, makin' blanks outa them. But it was fired this mornin'. Fella didn't bother to clean it good. I could smell the gunpowder."

Carmer spoke. "I fail to see that this is getting us anywhere. It's all pure speculation."

"Uh-huh," said Buchanan. "Only I checked some records. While Jackson was tendin' bar today. There was a package shipped in a couple months ago would just fit the description of a long-barreled Sharps rifle. The receipt for it was signed."

Nobody spoke; people were holding their breaths.

Buchanan said, "I also checked some bank accounts."

Oswald Owens started to speak, but he choked and shut his mouth.

"Bankers ain't allowed to talk about their depositors," said Buchanan. "So I just took a peek."

Bondi had stopped working at the manure and was trailing his pitchfork toward the barn, staring straight ahead in the manner of a deaf person. Hunt shifted his position. Coco came and stood near Hunt.

Buchanan lowered his voice. "Would you believe, folks, that a man runnin' a sloppy little old business in this town could bank, on two separate and distinct occasions, two hundred dollars? The dates? Just after Buster and Gabe were murdered."

Bondi crouched. He held the pitchfork at waistlevel, aimed it at Buchanan and charged.

Buchanan shouted, "I want him alive."

Hunt held the gun at ear level. Coco poised on his toes. Bondi continued to run at Buchanan.

Buchanan waited until the last possible second. Then he sidestepped. He seized Bondi by the neck and twisted him around. Bondi ran into the wall of the stable. The prongs of the pitchfork penetrated and stuck. Coco gently hit Bondi behind the ear.

Buchanan had turned like a big cat. Carmer, Stremple and Oliver had not moved.

"Tie him up," Buchanan said. "He signed for the Sharps . . . Now, the question is, who paid him the money to kill?"

Carmer's eyes were shifting: to the street, to Buchanan, to the jury. He did not speak.

Buchanan said, "Who had a reason to kill Buster . . . Gabe . . . me . . . or Pat?"

He let them think this over. Brows were furrowed as the truth began to sink into minds.

Buchanan said, "Buster was a GG Ranch old-timer. Maybe he knew somethin' before any of us. Gabe — well, he was the big man around here. Some people thought Lazy M wanted to get rid of Gabe. That's what the killer wanted them to think. That's why Hunt was set up for the killin' of Fred Masters, to turn people against Lazy M."

He paused again. He wasn't used to talking like this in front of a lot of people, and he had many things on his mind. He moved again, standing beside the barrel. He was wearing his six-gun, but again he was fearful that bystanders would be hurt.

"It wasn't Lazy M who did it," he said. "I looked up another account in the bank. There were two withdrawals of two hundred dollars at the time Bondi was paid off."

He didn't like the way Carmer took it. Something was up. A sixth sense which warned of danger buzzed inside him. He decided to move fast.

"It was Vic Carmer who drew the money. It was Vic Carmer who hired the killin's." He said it loud and clear.

They came from the street. Mary Goodwin, her hair streaming, her eyes unfocused, led them. She had managed to get the three gunmen out of the unattended jail, and Buchanan cursed himself for the oversight which had allowed it to happen.

They were all western people; they hit the dirt. Then the guns began to roar.

Buchanan, knowing of the hidden derringer, was watching Carmer's belt. The saloonkeeper raised his left hand and fired pointblank. Buchanan winced as the heavy bullet tore out a piece of his shoulder. Hunt was firing from the stable wall. McKay and the Lazy M men were shooting as fast as they could. Stremple had a six-gun in both hands and was aiming at Buchanan.

Because Carmer's shot staggered Buchanan, Stremple's first bullet missed, Buchanan ducked and ran. He got hold of Carmer as the second shot from the derringer plowed harmlessly into earth. He wheeled around, using Carmer as a shield, his hands around the man's throat.

He saw Mary coming at them. He tried to twist away. Carmer had the second hideout gun from the belt. Buchanan shook him like a terrier shaking a rat. Carmer got off one shot.

Mary threw up her hands and fell. Pat Goodwin ran to stand astride her, his six-gun working. The three gunmen were all hit now, Buchanan saw. Hunt had accounted for two of them. Coco had managed to get behind Stremple, and now he struck a mighty blow. Stremple went forward, his neck oddly twisted from the impact. Coco did not stop. He got to Oliver and dropped him with a one-two to the jaw. Buchanan tightened his grip on Carmer.

In less than a minute it was over. The silence that fell was profound. Not even the sparrows on the manure pile made a sound.

Finally Dr. Gill said, "I think you'd better let go, Buchanan. I think the man is dead." He went to attend to Mary Goodwin.

Buchanan dropped Carmer as though he were a sack of beans. He felt nothing. Destroying this conniver was not a matter on which to brood. He hated to kill, but the extermination of such a person could not touch him.

Hunt said, "I think we got a few corpuses. One of them buckeroo fancy gun hands put a bullet in Bondi."

It was true. The stableman lay with a hole in his skull. Buchanan anxiously looked around. People were regaining their feet. Scott McKay was picking Linda up.

"Nobody hurt except Mary, I think," Pat Goodwin said. "Poor Mary."

Linda ran to him and took his hand. "She's not well, she'll be all right. I saw her move."

Dr. Gill raised his head. "Take her to my place. She'll be a while getting well. But she'll do . . . by the grace of God."

Buchanan said, "If you could spare a hunk of bandage Doc, I can manage the rest."

Linda said, "You were hit! You're bleeding!"

"Uh-huh," Buchanan said. He accepted a roll of bandage from Dr. Gill. "Excuse me a minute."

He went into the stable with Coco and Hunt and took off his shirt. The two men stared at him, at his scars and amazing muscular development.

Hunt said, "And I wanted to kill a man built like that."

Coco took the bandage and began applying it with hands skilled through the long practice of his profession. He said, "Guns, always guns. That shootin' plumb scares me stiff."

"You did all right again," Buchanan said. "Hunt, it's all settled, you'll be the next sheriff."

"It's *loco,*" Hunt said. "But when a man gets a call . . . it's up to him to serve. I reckon. Heard some politician say it somewhere, sometime, at any rate."

Buchanan put his shirt back on. They went out into the yard, where people were cleaning up the mess. Oliver, coming to, was ready for jail. Strempl's neck was broken. The gunmen were all beyond repair. Carmer's face was blue: He had been strangled to death.

There was a clatter of hooves, and men rode into the yard. Buchanan looked up at the scowling features of Major Jones. Hunt stood his ground, as did Coco.

"What's going on here?" the major demanded. "What's this I hear about you refereeing a prizefight, Buchanan?"

Buchanan reached for his badge, unpinned it and handed it up to the major. "Yep. Reckon that finishes me. Before you fire me — I resign."

"What's all this other confusion? Have you thrown this entire town into a turmoil?"

Buchanan said mildly, "You might say so."

"I'll have all three of you in jail. I sent you up here to keep the peace. You're under arrest, Buchanan — and you two, also."

Buchanan said, "Major, you're a good man. Trouble with you is, you don't stay still long enough to get your reports. Or that dummy Wale don't give 'em to you. But before you turn the key on us, you better talk to some people. Like Banker Owens and Doc Gill and Basilio and Scott McKay and Pat Goodwin — and, oh, a whole heap of people. Meantime — how about you and me goin' over and arrestin' a man named Jackson and havin' a drink on the house?"

They rode out together, Buchanan and Coco Bean. They had money in their pockets, and they were heading for New Mexico and the Black Range. Nightshade was happy, snorting and acting up, with resultant twinges to Buchanan's sore shoulder. The six-guns were in the saddle roll, the rifle nestled in its scabbard.

Coco said, "Sure hope that arm gets better quick."

"Thanks," Buchanan said. "We sure got out of that rangdoodle lucky."

Coco said, "Guns . . . Yep, I sure hope it heals quick. One thing I hate is minin'."

"You don't have to ride along," Buchanan told him. "You're welcome, but nobody's forcin' you."

"I knows," Coco said. "But you forget somethin'."

"What do I forget?"

"Soon's that arm is okay, you and me got somethin' to settle. I still don't believe you can beat me in no fair fight."

"Uh-huh," Buchanan said. He sighed. It was ever thus. Life was just one challenge after another. A man tried to meet them all. It was really tough to try and be peaceable in a country of violent people. Heaven knew that he tried . . .

William R. Cox was born in Peapack, New Jersey. His early career was in newspaper journalism. In the late 1930s he began writing sports, crime, and adventure stories for the magazine market, and he made his debut as a Western writer with "Night of the Blood Bucket Raid" in *Dime Western* in the January, 1941 issue. It is worth noting that his Western story debut was with the first of several stories to feature a series character, Terry Glenn. During the 1940s Cox created a number of other series characters for the magazine market, most notably the Whistler Kid who appeared regularly in *10 Story Western* and Duke Bagley whose adventures usually were featured in *Star Western*. "The short story form was blissful until there were no markets," he once recalled. In the 1950s and 1960s Cox turned to television and wrote at least a hundred teleplays for such series as "Broken Arrow," "Dick Powell's Zane Grey Theatre," "The Virginian," and "Bonanza." He also won a host of readers writing original paperback Western novels, the best known of which are novels about the adventures of two series characters originally published by Fawcett Gold Medal: Cemetery Jones in a series published under his own byline and the Tom Buchanan series which appeared under the house name, Jonas Ward. Dale L. Walker in the second edition of TWENTIETH CENTURY WESTERN WRITERS commented that William R. Cox's Western "novels are noted for their 'pageturner' pace, realistic dialogue, and frequent Colt-and-Winchester gun play. The series of novels built around the strong West Texas character, Tom Buchanan, are very typical Cox Westerns."

The employees of G.K. Hall & Co. hope you have enjoyed this Large Print book. All our Large Print titles are designed for easy reading, and all our books are made to last. Other G.K. Hall Large Print books are available at your library, through selected bookstores, or directly from us.

For information about titles, please call:

(800) 223-2336

To share your comments, please write:

Publisher
G.K. Hall & Co.
P.O. Box 159
Thorndike, Maine 04986